Looking over at the gathering, Daniel saw that more than one man and woman had noticed them standing together. He was damaging her reputation.

"You need to walk away from me right now."

"I think not."

He tried again. "People are going to talk."

Lela shrugged. "People talk no matter what. I'm used to it, anyway."

The young woman—likely barely twenty—was beautiful. She had on a pale blue dress, her *kapp* covered shiny brown hair, and her cheeks were plump and pleasing. Added to that, she was proper and sweet. Her dark brown eyes also seemed to see more than most anyone else.

Unable to help himself, he asked, "Why would you be used to people talking about you?"

"Because of my cousin, of course."

He still wasn't following. "I'm sorry?"

"You know who he is, right? My cousin was Brandt Showalter. He's the boy everyone said you killed."

Shelley Shepard Gray writes inspirational and sweet contemporary romances for a variety of publishers. With over a million books in print, and translated into more than a dozen languages, her novels have reached both the *New York Times* and the *USA TODAY* bestseller lists. Shelley's novels have also been featured in a variety of national publications.

In addition to her writing, Shelley has hosted several well-attended Girlfriend Getaways for Amish reading fans. Her most recent Girlfriend Getaway, hosted with several other novelists, was highlighted on Netflix's *Follow This* series.

Before writing romances, Shelley taught school and earned her bachelor's degree in English literature and later obtained her master's degree in educational administration. She now lives in southern Colorado near her grown children, walks her dachshunds, bakes too much and writes full-time.

Also by Shelley Shepard Gray

Inspirational Cold Case Collection

Widow's Secrets
Amish Jane Doe

Visit the Author Profile page
at Harlequin.com for more titles.

AMISH FUGITIVE

SHELLEY SHEPARD GRAY

LOVE INSPIRED
INSPIRATIONAL ROMANCE

LOVE INSPIRED®
INSPIRATIONAL ROMANCE

Recycling programs
for this product may
not exist in your area.

ISBN-13: 978-1-335-46838-3

Amish Fugitive

Copyright © 2023 by Shelley Sabga

For questions and comments about the quality of this book, please contact us at CustomerService@Harlequin.com.

Love Inspired
22 Adelaide St. West, 41st Floor
Toronto, Ontario M5H 4E3, Canada
www.LoveInspired.com

Printed in U.S.A.

For if our heart condemn us, God is greater than our heart, and knoweth all things.
—*1 John* 3:20

What lies behind us and what lies before us are tiny matters compared to what lies within us.
—Amish Proverb

For Tom, who not only walked through a corn maze with me but didn't blink an eye when I decided to see if it was actually possible to hide in one, too.

Chapter One

September

Daniel Darrel Miller had stayed at the luncheon as long as he'd dared. Against his brother Abram's wishes, he'd attended the church service at the Zooks' house. It wasn't like he'd had much choice. If he hadn't gone, everyone would say that he was just as bad as they'd thought he was.

He couldn't afford to make things worse for himself than they already were. Within the first ten minutes, however, he'd regretted his decision.

Though no one had attempted to make him leave, it was more than obvious that he wasn't welcome. Even Abram and his wife, Sylvia, had kept their distance, as if they'd needed to prove to everyone in their church district that, while they were good enough to give him shelter, they didn't much want to have anything to do with Abram's younger brother.

Making things worse, Abram had cast several dark

looks in his direction when the three-hour Sunday service was over. It was clear he wanted Daniel to leave.

That stung, though Daniel reckoned he shouldn't be asking for more than Abram had already given him. With their parents gone to Heaven and their sister Violet in Indiana, his brother hadn't had much choice about what to say when both a lawyer and Daniel himself had called to ask if he could stay with them for a spell. Just until Daniel got back on his feet.

Unfortunately, it was very apparent that Abram and Sylvia were counting the hours until Daniel walked back out of their lives. If their situations were reversed, he might even feel the same way.

Deciding that there was only so much a man could do to repair damage that had taken years to develop, Daniel knew it was time to go. The moment he finished the sandwich, potato salad and apple that had been provided, he got to his feet, carefully set his plate and fork in the dish tub provided and forced himself to go over to where Isaac Zook was sitting. The man was with Bishop Joe Schlabach and Elam Borntrager. The three of them were in deep conversation, and common courtesy demanded that he wait until they were finished before he approached. Five minutes turned to ten and then fifteen. More and more people cast sideways looks in his direction. He could practically feel their disdain for him grow.

He really wished he could leave.

Unfortunately, common courtesy also demanded that Daniel thank the host of Sunday's service before he left. Even though he felt as if every single person in the vicinity was looking at him in disapproval, he moved near the trio.

When he came to a stop in front of them, all three men grew silent.

"Jah?" Isaac said after a second's pause.

Daniel glanced at the bishop. Drawing strength from the kind man's encouraging expression, he cleared his throat. "I'm sorry to interrupt your conversation, Isaac. I only wanted to thank you for your hospitality."

Instead of thawing, the man looked even more ill at ease. "There's no need for you to thank me. I'm only doing what is expected. Each of us must host services twice a year."

He'd been put in his place. Trying to think of an appropriate response, Daniel stuffed his hands in his pockets. "Yes. Well…" His voice drifted off as his mind went blank. What in the world was the appropriate response, anyway?

When the strained silence lingered, Isaac turned away. Elam Borntrager, on the other hand, continued to stare at him as if he was an unwanted rodent in their midst.

The rejection hurt, but it was no less than he expected. Furthermore, it wasn't as if Daniel could blame him. It was because of Daniel that Elam had lost his nephew.

Taking comfort in the fact that he'd mastered a carefully blank expression, he stepped back. Obviously there was nothing more to say.

Just as Daniel turned to go, the bishop spoke.

"Did you enjoy the service, Daniel?"

"I did." Well, he had as much as it had been pos-

sible. The morning's service had included Bishop Joe
and Preacher Josiah reading several verses from Deu-
teronomy. Each verse had cautioned each person to be
obedient to the Lord.

It had been a harsh set of sermons to listen to, especially since he had felt as if half the congregation was
glaring at him the entire time.

Bishop Joe smiled slightly. "Walk in peace, Daniel."

"*Danke*. You, as well."

Relieved that both the service and his duty were over,
Daniel turned and walked past the rest of the tables.
And the group of women sipping coffee and gossiping
next to the tray of cookies. And the batch of preschool-
ers chasing each other, each one laughing with greater
exuberance than the last.

Only when he reached the end of the drive did he
feel like he could breathe freely again. Realizing that he
was covered in a fine sheen of sweat—something that
hadn't happened since his first few months in prison—
he paused to inhale deeply.

"Are you all right?"

Startled, he turned on his heel. There, standing off
to the side of the driveway, partly hidden by the Zooks'
mailbox, was Lela Borntrager.

Lela was studying him with a look of concern. After
meeting her gaze, his mind went blank. They'd crossed
paths just a few days after he was released from prison.
He'd gone to the farmers market and had practically
knocked Lela over when he'd turned a corner too quickly.

Unfortunately, he'd then managed to make things
worse, since he'd been afraid to reach out to steady her
balance but also afraid to simply stand and watch her

stumble. He'd eventually grabbed her elbow. The assistance had been a few seconds too late but had helped Lela regain her footing.

Then she'd thanked him.

He'd been so struck by her sweetness, he'd continued to grasp her arm. After another five seconds passed, he'd jerked his hand away like his fingers were on fire.

When he dropped his hand, she'd smiled. That smile had been so pretty, he'd felt his whole being settle into place.

After that moment, he'd somehow kept seeing Lela around town. Every time, she'd made him feel flustered. He couldn't seem to help the way his heart responded whenever he came within three feet of her. Lela was lovely and kind, and that sweetness drew him in like a bee to honey.

Today was no different.

Embarrassed by his reaction, he looked down at his feet.

But instead of finding fault with that, she stepped closer. "Daniel, are you having trouble breathing? Do you need a cup of water?"

Her voice was like fairy dust. Or like spun sugar. Or anything else that was too fanciful to be real and too hard to ever hope to obtain. *"Nee,"* he said at last. His mouth went dry. *Had his voice just squeaked?*

Confusion filled her brown eyes. "No, you aren't having trouble breathing, or no, you don't need a cup of water?"

"No to both." Realizing that he sounded rude even to his own ears, he cleared his throat. "I mean, *nee*, but *danke*. I am fine."

To his surprise, Lela looked disappointed. "Oh. Well, I am glad about that."

When she didn't move away, he told himself to turn and start walking. But for some reason, he simply couldn't do it. It had been a really long time since he'd received so much kindness.

Of course, on its heels was another bout of worry and self-loathing. She shouldn't be around him, let alone sharing a private conversation. People would talk. After one second turned into two, then three, he said, "What are you doing out here, Lela?"

She lifted her chin. "Why shouldn't I be here?"

"Because everyone else is gathered together on the Zooks' lawn. Don't you want to be with the rest of the group?"

"Not especially." A hint of a smile lit up her face. "*Mei* parents like to stay as long as possible after the luncheons. I'm always ready to relax at home, though. It's the Lord's day, ain't so?"

He nodded. Lela wasn't wrong. Sundays were a day of rest. At least, they should be, he supposed. Of course, when he got home, he would clean the house for a while. Then he would likely go to the *dawdi haus* and clean that, too. It was not only expected, it was the least he could do. He owed his brother for taking him in.

Lela shifted. Folded her arms across her chest. "You sure don't say too much, Daniel. Have you always been that way? Or did you learn to be quiet in prison?"

Tossing out his resolve to remain carefully stoic and distant whenever she was near, Daniel gaped. "I can't believe you said that."

A line formed between her brows. "I'm sorry. Would

you feel better if no one ever mentioned your time in Mansfield? If so, I won't bring it up again."

Now he just felt foolish. As if never speaking about his past was going to somehow make it go away. "I didn't say you shouldn't mention prison. I was just surprised." When she simply stared at him, he added, "It don't really make a difference to me one way or the other."

"No?"

"It's where I was, whether folks mention it or not."

Lela seemed to think about that for a moment before replying. "That's how the past is, don't you think?" she mused. "No matter how hard one might try to paint it a different color, it's always with us."

"I reckon so." Looking over at the gathering, Daniel saw that more than one man and woman had noticed them standing together. One pair of women were staring at Lela curiously. He was damaging her reputation.

"You need to walk away from me right now."

"I think not."

He tried again. "People are going to talk."

Lela shrugged. "People talk no matter what. I'm used to it, anyway."

The young woman—likely barely twenty—was beautiful. She had on a pale blue dress, her *kapp* covered shiny brown hair, and her cheeks were plump and pleasing. Added to that, she was proper and sweet. Her dark brown eyes also seemed to see more than most anyone else.

Unable to help himself, he asked, "Why would you be used to people talking about you?"

"Because of my cousin, of course."

He still wasn't following. "I'm sorry?"

"You know who he is, right? My cousin was Brandt Showalter. He's the boy everyone said you killed."

Though what she said was correct, the bold statement still stung. He took a step backward. "Not everyone says that. I was acquitted."

Looking pained, she reached out and clasped his hand. "I know you were. Please forgive me. I didn't mean to sound as if I didn't know that. I… I get tired of everyone talking in circles and half-truths so I sometimes speak a bit too freely at times."

He stared at their hands. Her skin was soft and smooth. And cool. She wasn't gripping him. No, it was more like she sought to give comfort.

Goosebumps appeared on his arm. Daniel could almost feel his pulse quicken, too. All from just one innocent touch. He was embarrassed by his reaction, but he supposed he shouldn't have been. After all, this was the first time a woman had touched him in years.

"Lela?" Charity Borntrager's voice was clear and piercing. "Lela, what in the world are you doing?"

Looking stricken, Lela dropped her hand. "My *mamm* is heading our way. I'm so sorry, Daniel. I've got to go."

"I know you do."

He might be an innocent man who'd been framed for another man's murder. He might be attempting to reinvent himself and be seeking respect from his peers, but in the end, Lela was right. His past was always going to be with him.

Even if he hadn't shot the gun that had killed Brandt, he'd held it. And while Brandt had wanted to try new things during his *rumspringa*, he wouldn't have gone to the party if Daniel hadn't taken him. He'd even allowed Wyatt Troyer to speak to Brandt privately when he knew that was a dangerous thing to do.

So, yes. Yes, Lela really did need to stay far away from him. His reputation was too bad. He'd done too many things—both in prison and out—to deserve her sympathy.

When Lela remained where she was, still gazing at him like an avenging angel, Daniel knew what he had to do.

Without another word, he turned down the main road and started walking as fast as he dared. He needed to put as much distance between himself and Lela Borntrager as possible. Not just because of who she was and her relation to Brandt.

But because of the man he was now. In most ways, he simply wasn't fit for company.

Chapter Two

"Lela, when will you ever learn?" her mother muttered under her breath as she wrapped her hand around Lela's elbow and pulled her closer to her side.

Lela allowed herself to be pulled, but her patience with her mother's need to treat her like a wayward child was wearing thin. She didn't like being yanked around, and she was really too old to be receiving a lecture on the side of the road.

Pulling her arm away, she lifted her chin. "When will I learn what, *Mamm*."

With a sigh, her mother dropped her hand as she visibly attempted to regain some decorum. "You know exactly what I'm talking about."

Of course she did, but that didn't mean she was going to give credence to it. "Perhaps."

"Perhaps?"

"*Mamm*, I'm too old for you to be carting me around. I'm still not even sure why you came out to find me."

"You know why. Besides, I didn't have to hunt for you, the entire congregation saw you standing with him."

Lela had also mastered the art of looking at her mother directly in the eye whenever she began a lecture. It made *Mamm* uncomfortable, which usually caused her harangue to be far shorter than she intended.

Her eldest sister, Anna, had once chided Lela for being so brash. Lela had paid her no mind, though. As far as she was concerned, their mother's penchant for delivering long, fiery lectures accompanied by the shaking of her children's elbows wasn't very nice, either.

All that was why Lela took another step backward just in case her mother attempted to grab her again.

Mamm clasped her hands together.

Glad she wasn't about to be sporting another set of bruises on her arm, Lela smiled. "Did you need something, *Mamm*?"

"Do I need something? You know I do." Her mother's dark look turned thunderous. "What I need is an explanation." She held up a hand when Lela was about to play dumb. "And don't you start pretending you don't know what I'm referring to."

"I honestly don't. What did I do wrong now?"

"You were speaking to Daniel Miller, daughter."

"*Jah*. I know. I was speaking to Daniel in plain sight of the rest of our church community on a Sunday after listening to a solemn sermon about Christian duty. I did nothing wrong."

"What has gotten into you, Lela?" After furtively looking around, she lowered her voice. "You are going to ruin your reputation. Rumors might start."

"I canna control what the gossips say. If someone does spread rumors about me, that is their problem. Not mine."

"You are being naive on purpose. Stay away from that man."

"*That man* is not a criminal. Daniel was found innocent, *Mamm*."

"He's still tainted. He spent time in prison. You need to keep your distance from him. If you don't, our friends and neighbors might start to wondering about your character."

"Because I spoke to Daniel after church?" She didn't even try to hide her incredulousness.

"It's a woman's place to watch her reputation. Don't forget that."

Though it would be safer to keep her mouth closed, Lela couldn't do it. Her mother's criticism wasn't fair. Not anything even close to being fair. "I wasn't giving anyone anything to talk about. All I did was wish Daniel a good afternoon."

"We both know you did more than that. You were having a *conversation*. Likely everyone noticed."

"Likely everyone is also noticing that you are lecturing me right this minute." Unable to help herself, she raised an eyebrow. "Did you intend to do that, as well?"

Twin spots of color stained her mother's cheeks. "You are becoming so willful. I don't know why. Is it all the baby and dog sitting you're doing?"

"Mother, neither babies nor dogs make one willful."

"Well, something has made you far too full of yourself. It ain't good, Lela. It ain't good at all."

Neither was this conversation. "I helped clean up. I'm going home. I'll see you later."

"Who are you walking with?"

"No one.".

Stepping closer, she grabbed Lela's elbow and dug her fingers in deep. "You mustn't. It isn't safe."

Irritated that her mother had caught her by surprise, Lela pulled herself free. "Mamm, stop. You are hurting me!" And yes, she'd raised her voice on purpose.

Someone in the distance inhaled sharply.

Her mother dropped her hand, but continued to lecture. "Listen to what I am saying, child. Daniel Darrell Miller could be on the side of the road, just waiting for you."

At the moment, Lela rather hoped he was. "I don't believe he is."

"But he could be. I noticed the expression on his face. I think he might be thinking about you."

"I'm leaving, *Mamm*. Please, just let me be." She turned and started walking down the road before her mother was able to say another word.

It was at least a forty-five-minute walk, and she was grateful for the chance to do some real thinking about what to do for the rest of her life.

Of course, the answer was obvious. She was going to have to eventually accept one of the men's suits who had come calling, plan a wedding, get married and then hope and pray that she would get pregnant very soon.

Just as her three older sisters had done.

Lela wasn't against marriage or against being a mother. On the contrary, she wanted both of those things. She just didn't want to commit herself to any of the men who had shown interest in her. They were either too immature or carbon copies of their fathers.

They had expectations for a wife—most of which seemed unreasonable to her. Or, the men had specific views on most everything and expected Lela to adopt the very same opinions they had.

However, the worst part was that all the men tried to tell her what to do. Like she didn't have a perfectly good brain in her head. She'd made sure they'd realized that she wasn't the woman for them.

At first, her mother had been patient with Lela's courtship catastrophes. Now, unfortunately, both of her parents' patience was gone. Just last week, *Daed* had threatened to forbid her from baby and pet sitting until she acted more amenable to her suitors.

Not that she had many suitors left.

Needing the break her small jobs provided, Lela pretended to go along with her father's threats, but it was only a temporary bandage. If she didn't change her ways soon, her parents were going to change them for her.

"Hey there, Lela."

She jumped. It was Rebecca Simon. She was an *Englischer* and one of Lela's favorite customers. She had a fluffy golden retriever named Belle who was a sweetheart and could do all kinds of tricks.

Quickly composing herself, Lela smiled. "Hi, Rebecca. How are you?"

"I'm well. I decided to go out for a long walk. It's a beautiful day, isn't it?"

"It is, indeed. Where's Belle? I'm surprised she isn't by your side."

"She would have come, but John is home from college. She's sleeping on the end of his bed." Rebecca smiled, showing that she completely understood that the dog was happy to see her son.

Plus, that was life at Rebecca's house. Belle was a

pampered dog, and Rebecca's two college-aged children were pampered, too. Lela bit back a moment of longing. She didn't necessarily yearn to be spoiled, but she wouldn't have minded being coddled a bit every now and then.

"You look pretty, dear. What have you been doing today?"

"I was just at church. You know how we Amish go to each other's houses for church. We had services and then lunch. Now I'm walking home."

Rebecca frowned. "It's quite a ways. Do you need a ride? As you know, I just live down the street. I'm happy to take you home."

"Thank you, but I like walking on my own. It gives me time to think."

"I feel the same way." Her phone beeped. "Although it looks like my sister is trying to get through to me. I better call her back. I'll reach out to you soon about watching Belle."

"*Danke*. Have a nice day."

Lela continued on, half thinking about upcoming jobs and half thinking about Daniel Miller and how he'd acted when he'd learned that she was Brandt's cousin. He'd looked upset and full of remorse. Like she shouldn't even be talking to him.

Glancing to her right, she saw a phone shanty and Daniel himself standing outside of it. Even though they were easily ten yards away from each other, he met her gaze.

She stopped. Raised her hand and waved.

For a few seconds, Daniel did nothing. Then, after

a little hesitation, he waved back. Right before he turned away.

As she walked on, Lela smiled to herself. Already, they'd made a little bit of progress. Maybe a friendship between the two of them wasn't an impossibility after all.

Chapter Three

The fact that the case file was thin should've been Detective Nate Borntrager's first clue that it hadn't been handled well. Thoroughly conducted investigations contained lots of notes, lots of pictures and a lengthy list of witnesses and suspects who were interviewed. Some ended up being two inches thick. Brandt Showalter's file wasn't even an inch.

Thinking back to the days surrounding his nephew's death, guilt hit Nate hard. He'd should've done more for the boy. Nate had intended to help as much as he legally could without interfering, but Brandt's murder had taken place during an especially difficult time in his life. He'd been in the middle of a divorce, as well as his own homicide investigation. An elderly woman had been killed in a home invasion. A pair of addicts had broken into her house looking for both prescription drugs and valuables. Eighty-year-old Hazel Jornigan had neither of those things. She'd been a spry widow who still walked three miles a day and didn't believe in going to the doctor.

Her senseless death, combined with the exorbitant sum his lawyer was charging during the divorce proceedings, had been all he'd thought about. Though he'd mourned Brandt's death and had reached out to his sister Amy and brother-in-law Floyd, they'd made it extremely clear that they hadn't wanted his support. Even when he'd offered to help them understand some of the legal terms, Floyd had refused. Floyd didn't trust anyone who jumped the fence. That had hurt, but he hadn't wanted to press.

Because he had so many other things tugging on all his time and energy, Nate had listened to Amy and stayed out of the loop. When Michael Peck, the detective in charge of the case, had closed it easily, Nate had been relieved that not only had justice been served but that he hadn't had to get involved.

After a year passed, both Floyd and Amy had died. Floyd of an apparent stroke and Amy of an infection that she'd refused to seek medical help for. He'd attended both funerals, but he hadn't stayed for the meals at either. He was too far removed from the insulated world, and most people only seemed to eye him with suspicion.

Over time, Nate had almost comforted himself with the knowledge that it really was impossible to go back home again. His former schoolmates and relatives seemed to view him as an outsider. It would likely always be that way.

But then several months ago, a group of college students had decided to champion Daniel Miller's cause. Within just a couple of weeks, Daniel Darrel Miller had been deemed innocent.

Nate felt terrible about the whole situation. Not only

had Brandt's killer not been found, but an innocent Amish boy had been tried as an adult and sentenced to prison. His life was probably ruined.

Walking over to Detective Peck's desk, he said, "Got a minute, Mike?"

The friendly grin on Mike's face turned wary as he noticed what was in Nate's hand. "Sorry, but I'm pretty busy right now."

"This won't take long."

Mike slid his chair away from his desk with a sigh. "Is this about that Amish kid's death again?"

"If you're talking about my nephew Brandt, yes."

"We already had a talk with Captain Ward when the Miller kid got out. You didn't have any questions then. You need to drop it now."

Aware that Mike's tone and belligerent attitude was attracting some of the others' notice, Nate mentally shook his head. There were other reasons Mike hadn't received either much of a pay raise or a promotion: he was filled with too much pride and he wasn't very smart. It was a bad combination for a cop.

With effort, Nate held his cool. He was just as much to blame as anyone else. Though he wouldn't have been allowed to be involved, he still should've asked more questions.

"I took another look at the file, and I'm wondering if maybe some of your notes might have fallen out or something." It was unlikely, but he didn't want to make an enemy of the detective.

"Everything's there." Folding his arms over his chest, he added, "You know better than me that no Amish kids—or their parents—would give me the time of day."

He shifted uncomfortably. "Besides, back then everyone agreed that it had to be Daniel Darrel Miller. He'd been drinking and been running wild for months. Plus, the kid didn't even try to get out of it. He basically sat silently every time I tried to get some answers out of him. I could've gotten more information from a rock."

"He might not have understood everything you were saying, Mike. English was his second language."

"He could speak just fine."

"He only had an eighth grade education and it doesn't cover legal terms."

"He had a public defender." When Nate was about to say something about that, Mike's manner turned even more prickly. "I'm not going to sit here and defend myself to you, Nate. It's a little late for that, right?"

"No."

"Come on. You were around back then. Even though you wouldn't have been allowed to be in the thick of things, you sure didn't question a single thing I did. Let's stop pretending that you were super concerned—because you weren't."

"I'm going to take on my nephew's case. I just wanted you to know."

"Fine. Whatever." He made a shooing motion with his hand. "Just leave me out of it. I've got enough work on my plate right now."

"I see that." Irritated with both Mike's attitude and himself, he walked back to his desk in a separate room. The police station was fairly small, but filled with a lot of rooms. He shared a room with another detective on the force, Jill Pavelich. She was a middle-aged woman with three years seniority in the department.

She looked up as he neared. "I would ask how the conversation went, but judging from the expression on your face, I'm guessing not well."

"You'd guess right." He tossed the file on his desk. "Peck wasn't too inclined to help me out."

"I bet he wasn't." She rolled her eyes. "I've pretty much told Lieutenant McConnell that I'd rather direct traffic in a snowstorm than have to work side by side with that guy ever again."

"Whoa. He was that difficult?"

Jill tucked a chunk of gray hair behind an ear. "Difficult implies that Mike actually works hard. He does not. He's lazy as all get-out."

"I haven't had too many occasions to work with him in the past. When I did, though, I hadn't found him too difficult."

"That's because he didn't have anything to lose. Now that the guy's reputation is completely shot, he's feeling vulnerable." Jill pursed her lips. "Plus, it's not like anyone on the force is going to step up for him. He's burned a lot of bridges. I'm not the only person who thinks that, either."

Nate was feeling more and more dismayed. How could he have not known about all the scuttlebutt surrounding Michael Peck? Taking a seat next to Jill, he said, "I'm starting to think I need to pay more attention to what goes on around here."

Jill chuckled. "It's probably good you don't. You do better with people who can't talk back. Dead bodies and cold cases are your forte."

Which didn't say much about him. "Thanks," he replied in a dry tone.

She grinned. "Anytime."

Nate stared down at the folder he still held in his hands. "I'm going to take a few personal days and head over to Lodi."

"Do you think that's wise?"

He knew Jill was not just talking about the integrity of the case but also Nate's own personal feelings. "I don't think I have a choice. I need to do something to help not just Brandt but maybe even Daniel."

"Okay. But be careful, buddy."

He'd already shared with Jill not only that the victim was his nephew, but that he was former Amish himself. In addition, most officers knew that most of the population of Lodi was Swartzentruber Amish. They were the most conservative and aloof Amish communities—at least with outsiders. Getting information wasn't going to be easy.

"I will. But don't worry. I'll be fine."

After all, he didn't have a choice.

After much debate, Nate decided to touch base with his brother and sister-in-law before he started reaching out to the rest of the community. Or introduced himself to Daniel Miller. Elam Borntrager was a deacon in the church. He had a feeling that now—just like back when they were in school—Elam was having no problem finding fault with most everyone he'd come in contact with. Nate and Amy used to have a running joke that their brother Elam couldn't pass the most perfect rose without pointing out its thorns.

That said, Nate also realized that Elam likely knew most of the Amish in the area and would be a good re-

source. Nate didn't think Elam would willingly inter-
fere with his questions, but he did think that his brother
could make things more difficult for him if he wasn't
on his side.

As he approached his brother's house on the gravel
drive, Nate felt his mouth go dry. Everything looked
even worse than he remembered. Charity and Elam
looked determined to take living Plain very seriously.

And, in the way Elam did most things, he went to
extreme measures. Their white clapboard house was
worn looking and run-down. Few shrubs or flowers
dotted the outside. The barn was a faded red. Weeds
poked out from where the sides of the structure met
hard dirt. The windows were covered with shades and
the door was tightly shut. All in all, it was very much
like the home he grew up in, and almost ten times more
desolate looking.

The home that he, Elam, Amy and their two other
siblings grew up in had always been a lively place.
While it hadn't been the happiest of homes, it was far
from the solemn, dark place that his brother and sister-
in-law seemed to have embraced.

Reminding himself not to judge, Nate knocked on the
door and mentally prepared to talk to either his brother
or Charity. Instead, their youngest daughter answered.

She was a beauty, for sure and for certain. It was like
the Lord himself had decided to intervene in Elam's
purposely gray world by giving the couple her.

"Hi. It's Lela, right?" At her faint nod, he added,
"I'm Nate." When she didn't respond, he added, "Nate
Borntrager."

"I'm sorry, who?"

He wasn't sure why he was surprised by her confusion but he was, all the same. "I'm your uncle. I'm your father's youngest brother."

Her eyes widened. "Oh." Obviously unsure about his appearance on her doorstep, she didn't move.

Since he was obviously a stranger, he didn't blame her…but the realization that he'd been essentially forgotten still stung all the same. "I stopped by to say hello to your parents. Is your father around?"

"*Nee*. Neither of my parents are." Peering out behind him, she squinted at the sun. "It's hot out here. Would you like a glass of water?"

"I would. Thank you."

"Please follow me." After closing the screen door behind him, he followed Lela down the dark hall. Even with his sunglasses off, it took Nate a moment to adjust to the darkness of the home. He wondered if the shades were kept down in order to keep the house cool——or to prevent unwanted eyes from peering into the windows.

"Here you are." Lela set a mason jar filled with water in front of him.

He took a sip. There was no ice and the water wasn't even all that cold. However, it was wet and did the job. Sipping again, he drained about half its contents. "*Danke*."

She nodded. "Why are you here?"

If he hadn't grown up Amish he might have been taken aback by her direct question. Instead, he appreciated her candidness. "Yeah, I guess it's obvious that I wouldn't come over without a good reason. I'm here for a couple of days to get more information about Brandt's death."

A line formed between her brows. "Why?"

Treading carefully, he elected to start with the most obvious reason first. "Well, first of all, I'm a cop, so it's my job. Secondly, even though I might not be Amish, Brandt was my nephew. I need to discover who killed him." He paused, uncertain whether to continue or to stop. He didn't want to shock her.

"You don't think Daniel killed Brandt, either?"

He shook his head. "The DNA evidence is irrefutable. Daniel absolutely did not murder Brandt."

"A lot of people think he must have, since he went to prison."

"A mistake was made. The courts rectified that. Daniel is innocent." Unable to hide the emotion in his voice, he added, "He always was, Lela. In my mind, there wasn't one but two tragedies that took place the night Brandt was killed. Brandt was a victim of a senseless murder, and Daniel was framed for it. Daniel Miller should have never gone to prison."

Lela stared at him for a long moment before seeming to come to a decision. "I want to help."

"You do?"

"Jah. I mean, if I can." She closed her eyes. "I mean, if I may."

Nate wondered if she was asking him for permission to get involved or was thinking about her father granting it to her. No matter, the answer was the same. "A police investigation isn't for you. Even though Brandt and Daniel were both victims, I know there's a good chance they might have been doing some things during their *rumspringa* you might find shocking."

He was being sincere. Some of the things he was going to find out were likely ugly. No way did he want that to taint her innocence. Even after all this time, he experienced plenty of sleepless nights spurred by some of the things he'd seen.

To his surprise, she didn't back down. "I knew Brandt. Better than you, I reckon."

"I'm sure you did."

Lela looked surprised that he'd agreed with her statement so easily. After a moment, she lifted her chin. "I also know more people around here than you do."

"Again, that is true. However, it could be dangerous, Lela. A can of worms might be opened."

Her eyes brightened. "A can of worms, hmm?"

"I'm not kidding."

The door opened and Charity stepped inside. "Lela, what in the world are you doing in the kitchen? You know you shouldn't—Nate?"

His sister-in-law was staring at him like she'd seen a ghost. "Hiya, Charity."

Inhaling sharply, she stared at him. Then grabbed her daughter's arm. "You shouldn't have let him inside, Lela."

"Mei uncle was thirsty."

"That is beside the point. No matter what, you really shouldn't be speaking to him."

"Why not? He's my uncle, *Mamm*."

Charity's voice lowered. "Go outside, Lela. Go outside and tend to the garden."

Still eyeing his sister-in-law's rough handling of Lela, every protective instinct he possessed reared. "Charity, calm down and let the poor girl have her arm back."

"Nate—"

"I mean it. I'm not going to stand here and watch you jerk her around."

Lela's eyes widened when her mother finally dropped her hand.

Noticing that Lela was rubbing her arm, he softened his tone. "Are you okay?"

She nodded.

"Sure?"

"I am sure, Nate."

"All right, then." Turning to Charity, he said, "I came here to talk to Elam. All Lela did was tell me that he wasn't home and offer me a glass of water. She hasn't done anything wrong."

Charity folded her arms across her chest. "What did you need to speak to your brother about? Nathan, what are you doing here?"

"Uncle Nate is asking about Brandt, *Mamm*."

Charity's already cautious expression turned fearful. Her bottom lip trembled before she visibly contained herself. "Go outside, child. Now."

Lela met Nate's eyes before turning and walking outside. The moment she crossed the threshold, Charity closed the door. "Nate, you might be pretending that you have a reason to be here, but we both know better. You should not be speaking with Lela."

"First, she's my niece, not a stranger. You know I would never hurt her, Charity." When her expression didn't change, he added, "You do realize that, right?"

Uncertainty wavered in her expression before she nodded. "That's still no reason for you to visit."

Well, that stung, but whatever. "Okay, how about this? I'm here because I'm trying to get justice for Brandt."

"Brandt's killer was identified. That Daniel Miller might think he can walk around our town like he's a free man, but we all know better. He was found guilty and put in jail."

"He was innocent. An innocent man was put in jail for a crime he didn't commit." Confused by her venomous tone, he added, "Where is your compassion? Why are you finding it so hard to forgive Daniel?"

"There's no reason to forgive him. He's—"

He finished her sentence before she spewed more hate. "He's innocent. The DNA tests prove it. You should be more charitable, Charity." And yes, he'd used that descriptor on purpose.

For a moment, his sister-in-law looked doubtful, but then pulled herself up straight again. "Don't speak to me about compassion or forgiveness. You need to leave my property and don't come back. Don't you speak to Lela again, neither."

"Charity, do you hear what you're saying? Lela is my niece. We're family."

Charity shook her head. "You aren't Amish. You don't have a relationship with her."

"I'd like one. How about that?"

Uncertainty flickered in her expressive eyes again before she visibly pushed it away. "It's not possible. If Brandt's father, Floyd, was still alive, I know he would never agree to you returning to our community. You shouldn't be talking to any of us. Especially not Lela."

Why especially not Lela? Was it because of her age… or for another reason? "Don't you think you're being a little closed-minded? I wasn't shunned, Charity."

"The bishop might have not had the nerve to shun

you, but as far as we're concerned, you're a stranger. Nate, you've become a man with different values and a different life than the one we've chosen to live. The only thing your presence is going to do is stir things up that should be left alone. Let the past stay in the past."

As far as Nate was concerned, things needed to be stirred up. But just as he opened his mouth to tell her that, he finally understood the reason behind her gruff exterior.

Charity was afraid.

Of what, he wasn't sure, but there was no doubt that the fear was real.

Nate walked back down the dim hallway, unlatched the screen door and finally headed to his car. He glanced around the yard, hoping to catch sight of Lela, but she was nowhere to be found.

Just as he reached his Jeep, he heard the front door shut. Essentially removing him from their lives.

Nate knew better, however.

Getting rid of something unwanted wasn't easy to do. It never had been. He was living proof of that.

Chapter Four

It was Thursday afternoon. To Daniel's relief, the day had dawned sunny and the temperatures were expected to stay in the low eighties. While some of the men at Carter and Sons Construction could work on roofs in any sort of weather, Daniel wasn't one of them. He was still nervous being up so high, and the tether attached to the band around his waist didn't make him feel any safer.

However, as his coworkers had promised, his fears about falling had lessened. Experience and lots of prayers were making each job easier.

So, the day had gone well. Even better news was the fact that he was making progress. He was grateful for that. He didn't mind working hard but he reckoned he liked relaxing on a couch as much as anyone.

"You good, Dan?" Zeke, his crew leader, called out from down below.

In the middle of situating another patch of shingles, Daniel glanced down to the ground. Zeke was looking up at him in concern.

"*Jah*, I'm *gut*." He was doing as well as he could expect, he reckoned.

Instead of looking pleased, Zeke frowned. "Are you sure? You've been up there for three hours. It might be time for a break."

Once he was down on the ground he wanted to stay there. "I'm sure. Thank you."

Zeke didn't look like he completely believed him, but he nodded. "All right, then. But come down within thirty. Even though it isn't all that hot today, it does get warm up there. That tar paper absorbs heat like nobody's business. You've got to pace yourself. And don't forget to drink some Gatorade." Just as Daniel was about to protest that he could handle the job just fine, Zeke added, "The last thing anyone wants is for you to get dizzy or hurt. Then it will be my job to figure out how to get you safely down."

Whether Zeke was being completely truthful or making a joke, Daniel felt the tension in his muscles relax. His crew leader was right. No one was going to give him a prize for staying on top of a roof the longest—or for forcing Zeke to save his skin. "I'll be down shortly."

He was coming to learn that no roof felt small when one was balanced on its top and nailing shingles in, one at a time.

Beside him, Abraham laughed. "I figured Zeke telling you that he didn't want to make a rescue would get you to listen to him."

Daniel grinned. "Is it really a concern? Or does Zeke just send warnings in order to scare a fella?"

"Oh, it happens from time to time. These roofs are unforgiving." He shuddered. "I hate putting on shingles."

After nailing another section, he scooted over to get another batch of shingles. "It ain't my favorite, either."

Abraham whistled low. "We should go out and celebrate when we get off. At long last, you've finally complained about something."

"It wasn't a complaint. Not exactly."

"It was close enough to one," Abraham retorted, still obviously having a good time teasing him. "I was starting to think that you weren't human like the rest of us."

"I'm human." What Daniel wasn't, however, was ungrateful. When he'd first returned to Lodi, he'd felt like the worst sort of outcast. Everyone looked at him like he was contemplating murdering them in their sleep. Zeke Carter of Carter and Sons had been the only one to offer him a job. A decent job with good pay. After having to live inside behind bars for the majority of the last two years, he was actually pleased to have a job where he could be outside. "It's just… Well, this is a lot better than the work I did at the prison."

Abraham put down his hammer and drank a big swallow of water from the Igloo cooler perched on one of the completely flat areas of the roof. "Was it terrible, being in Mansfield?"

"*Jah*, it was." Daniel didn't particularly like talking about his time in prison, but he wasn't adverse to answering questions about it. Honestly, some days he ached to share his stories, not because he wanted someone to feel sorry for him, but because he felt the need to get the memories out. He still woke up a couple of times a month with his hands in tight fists, sure that he was back in his cell.

"What was the worst part?"

He didn't even have to think about his answer. "Never being alone."

"Really?" He sounded shocked, and Daniel supposed he didn't blame him.

"*Jah*. There was no privacy. The other prisoners look at you, looking for signs of weakness, and the guards... well, they're so sure you're worthless, you never get the benefit of the doubt." Or their help. A wave of nausea hit his stomach. Things had been very bad until he'd learned to fight.

Oblivious to his dark thoughts, Abraham grunted. "That makes sense, though, right? I mean, everyone there did something wrong."

"That is true, unless one is falsely accused," he said.

"Sorry."

Though Abraham had sunglasses on, it was easy to see that he was embarrassed by his words.

Daniel shrugged. "Don't worry about it none. I know you didn't mean anything by it." He paused, then said softly, "I promise, I'd rather be like you and have no idea what life in prison was like."

"I'm sorry you do."

"Danke." He didn't want to dwell on what had happened—he had done that enough.

They worked another half hour in silence. Daniel enjoyed being able to quiet his thoughts and listen to the faint chatter of a pair of robins nearby.

"Come on down, guys," Zeke called up.

Daniel got to his feet, slipped his hammer in his tool belt, then followed Abraham to the ladder. The first time he'd climbed down from a roof he'd had a bit of a scare, but now he hardly thought about it. Of course, he had a harness and a tether attached so he couldn't fall down easily, but the mind played tricks on a person. Sometimes it wasn't what could happen—it was dwelling on all the things that could be imagined.

When they were back on solid ground, Zeke tossed him a Gatorade. "Drink this and go sit in the shade for fifteen minutes."

"Danke." Seeing that Abraham was already relaxing under an oak tree, Daniel sat down beside him.

"It feels good to sit, right?"

"Jah." He took off his hat and smoothed back his hair, frowning when he realized how damp it was. "I guess I was sweating out there more than I realized."

Abraham nodded. "I've been doing this job for five years. I'd rather work with the sun on my back instead of the rain or wind in my face, but it ain't easy."

Daniel shuddered. "I'm not anxious to go up there in the rain."

"You shouldn't be. It ain't fun. Hey, I've been meaning to ask you where you're living. Where are you at?"

"I'm living with my brother, Abram."

"Do you like living there?"

He shrugged. "It's not like I have much of a choice. I didn't have any other option when I was released. Why do you ask?"

"Well, my missus and I decided to rent out our garage apartment. I thought you might be interested."

"I might be." Actually, the offer sounded like a huge blessing...but he knew better than to expect too much.

His buddy looked pleased. *"Jah?* That would be real good if you were. I want to rent it to someone I know and trust."

"What's it like?"

"Well, calling it an apartment might be overstating things a bit, but it ain't all bad. It's only one room, but it's a pretty good space. There's a sofa, double bed and a little kitchen with seating at the bar. A full bathroom, too."

"It sounds real nice." No, it sounded amazing. He'd never slept in a bed bigger than a twin, and having so much room for his six-foot frame would be appreciated. Then, too, was the added bonus of having so much space.

Abraham didn't realize it, but he wasn't used to having a lot of space anymore. His cell had been exactly that—a prison cell. Living back at home was so uncomfortable because of his brother and sister-in-law's resentment. He felt like it was his own prison.

When he didn't add anything else, Abraham said, "The apartment also has its own separate entrance. You'll have your privacy. Margaret and I won't be knocking on your door or anything like that."

"Isn't Margaret in a family way?"

"Yeah. She's due in five months. Why?"

"No reason." Other than he'd been fairly sure that Abraham wouldn't trust a man who'd been in prison around his wife and unborn babe.

"Oh. Well, if you're not interested, no worries."

Daniel belatedly realized then that he'd just inadvertently hurt the other guy's feelings. As if he thought a garage apartment wasn't good enough or something. "I am. I mean, I might. How much do you want a month?"

After naming the amount, Abraham added, "What do you think?"

"I think your price is less than I thought it would be." It was actually far less than he'd imagined.

Abraham shrugged. "Like I said, it ain't real big, and while I like the bit of extra money it brings in, I'm picky about who is there."

"To be honest, it sounds perfect."

"Yeah?" Abraham smiled. "That's great. Want to come over tomorrow and look at it?"

"I do. Thank you. I'm grateful."

"You're doing me a favor. I told my Margaret that I was hoping you'd take me up on the offer. It's always better to rent to someone you know, right?"

Once again, he was humbled by Abraham's trust in him. It was humbling and made him think that maybe he hadn't been wrong to move back to Lodi. It seemed not everyone in the community hated him.

He was still thinking about the unexpected, very good turn of events four hours later. They'd worked another three hours then spent another hour cleaning the area.

After the home's owner paid Zeke, Zeke paid him and Abraham and sent them on their way. Abraham drove off, no doubt going home to tell Margaret his news.

Though Zeke had offered to give Daniel a ride, he'd refused it. He was only three miles from home and he didn't mind the walk. He had a lot on his mind, starting and ending with the possibility of a new place to live.

When he was about halfway there, on a near-empty stretch of road, a gray SUV slowed down beside him. When the driver rolled down his window, Daniel's nerves went on edge.

"Are you Daniel Miller?"

"Who wants to know?"

"My name's Nate Borntrager."

"Yes?" The last name sounded familiar, of course. But there were dozens of families in the area with the same last names.

"Brandt was my nephew."

A tight knot formed in his stomach. "What do you want?" As much as he felt sorry for the man, Daniel did not want to get yelled at on the side of the road after working on a rooftop all day.

"Listen, can we talk? I have some questions I'd like to ask you. I'm a cop and I've recently opened the case again."

"There's nothing I have to tell you. I was cleared of Brandt's murder."

"I realize that."

"The evidence proved I hadn't shot the gun. They'd found no residue from the pistol on my clothes or when they'd taken my prints." Why he was trying so hard to be believed, he didn't know. It wasn't like anyone in the justice system had believed him before.

"Look, can you stop for a moment? I promise, I'm not here to make your life harder. I'm here because I'd like your help."

Even though he didn't fully believe him, he still stopped.

"There ain't nothing I can help you with."

"There might be." Nate ran a hand through his hair. "Look, I know we don't know each other, and you have a lot of really good reasons not to trust anyone in law enforcement. But give me some time, anyway."

There was something in Nate's tone that caught his attention. Reminded him of just how much he'd ached for someone, anyone, to give him a chance. To actually hear what he was saying instead of pushing their agenda. "All right. When?"

"Now?"

"Not now. I'm a sweaty mess. I need a shower."

"How about I drive you to your place, wait while you shower and then take you out to dinner? We can talk then." He smiled slightly. "At the very least you'll get a free meal."

It was obvious that Nate wasn't going to give up, and just as obvious that it would be better to get the meeting over with instead of pushing it off.

His brother wasn't going to like Nate pulling up on their drive, but it wasn't like they were going to like him being there if Nate didn't. The only thing they would be happy about was if he was gone.

"All right."

Nate smiled in obvious relief. "Great. Get in."

Chapter Five

Everything about Daniel's body language proclaimed that he would rather be any other place in the world than talking to Nate in his vehicle. Though it wasn't like Nate had needed to read his posture and expressions in order to guess what he was thinking. The guy was very good at verbalizing what he thought.

If the younger man wasn't so prickly, Nate would've told Daniel that he was proud of him. In his line of work, he'd seen far too many men and women—from both sides of the law—break down after fighting years of stress. For Daniel to have survived a prison stint when he was innocent—and then even get himself a job and continue on? Well, it was not only impressive, he considered it a minor miracle.

"So, I guess you're working construction." Though it had been obvious, Nate still gestured to the tool belt that was on the floor next to Daniel's feet. He needed to build some kind of rapport with him if at all possible.

"Jah."

"How's it going?"

He shrugged. "Well enough. It's a job."

"Do you want to do something else?" Nate didn't have a lot of connections among the Amish, but he was willing to reach out to people who might.

"I don't have a choice about whether I want to do it or not. As far as everyone is concerned, I'm a murderer."

"I'm sorry about that."

"It weren't your fault." Thawing slightly, he shrugged. "For the most part, I like construction and the job well enough. The work affords me the chance to be outside, and the other men I'm working with seem to be fair and good-tempered."

"That's a blessing."

Daniel studied Nate. "I don't understand why you came to find me. Were you involved in the first investigation?"

"I wasn't. Because I'm Brandt's uncle, my association could have tainted the case."

"Ah."

"Yeah." Whenever Nate thought about the work that Michael Peck had done, and his subsequent attitude even after it became obvious that Daniel was innocent, Nate's blood boiled. No cop was infallible. He wished Mike would man up and simply admit that he'd made some mistakes.

But so far, the other detective was so intent on keeping his job that he wasn't going to admit that any mistakes might have been made. All he kept saying was that it wasn't his fault he'd never turned in the fingerprints into the lab.

Worse, Daniel's public defender had been jaded and overworked. He hadn't done much for the young man besides show up in court. If the man had taken the time to thoroughly examine Daniel's case, he would've pointed out the shoddy police work.

That made Nate irritated. He'd learned early on in the police academy that though DNA and fingerprint databases were terrific resources, they couldn't take the place of good, old-fashioned police work. Mike should've dug into the case a whole lot more than he did.

But what grated on him—and several other officers—was the man's complete disregard for how his decisions affected victims, their families and the men and women who were accused or found to be innocent.

Like Daniel.

Feeling the young man's unusual hazel eyes searching his face, Nate cleared his throat. "Everyone's opinions about you will change when we find the real killer."

"You sound confident."

"I am. It might take me a while but I will do it."

"Do you think it's going to really be that easy?" Daniel asked after Nate parked on the gravel driveway of his house.

It took Nate a moment to understand what he was getting at. "Finding who really killed Brandt Showalter years ago? No."

"Nee," Daniel said as he unbuckled and opened the passenger door. "I mean reversing everyone's opinion of me."

"I don't think it will make your relationship with a lot of people around here automatically better," Nate replied as he got out of his vehicle and walked toward him. "That said, there's going to be a lot of people who will eventually begin to thaw. Right now, your innocence makes sense, but it's hard to believe. Even people who don't necessarily believe in the justice system don't like to imagine that it could go so wrong. However, when your naysayers see who really was at fault, they'll come around again."

"Maybe so."

Nate stepped closer, moving into Daniel's space. It gave the guy no choice but to stare back at him.

"Daniel, don't forget that I'm from here, too. I might have made the choice to become English and live in the city now, but that doesn't mean I don't care about the people here, or don't understand how things work. Most people have accepted me." Except for his own brother and sister-in-law, that was essentially true. They might not attempt to renew a relationship with him, but most of the Amish community were open-hearted.

Looking back at the cop, Daniel felt like rolling his eyes. Their situations were nothing alike, and it was irritating that this police detective was acting like they'd had similar histories. "You weren't in prison."

"You're right. I wasn't."

"Then you don't understand."

"I understand that you aren't the only person living in the area who feels that life isn't fair." When Daniel tried to interrupt, Nate held up a hand. "No, let me finish. You also aren't the only person concerned about you."

Thinking of Lela, Zeke, Abraham and even the woman at the coffee shop who teased him on Fridays, he nodded. "I reckon you're right."

Nate didn't budge. "Are you thinking of the Lord?"

Feeling like that question came out of nowhere, Daniel took a step backward. *"Nee."*

"I promise, He hasn't forsaken you."

He had never been the type of man to speak comfortably about his faith. "I know."

"Do you, though? Have you been talking to Him?"

"Not lately." When he'd been first accused, then charged with Brandt's murder, he'd talked to God a lot. He'd prayed and cried and then prayed harder. It didn't help.

"I love the Lord. I'm not saying that He doesn't create miracles. But He has absolutely not been by my side." Hating the hurt that was filling his insides, Daniel hardened his voice. "I don't know why."

To his surprise, Nate started laughing.

Irritated and hurt, Daniel lurched to his feet. "I think it's time for you to go."

"Hold on a sec. I'm not laughing at you." He stuck his hands in his pockets. "I mean, not really. It's just that, buddy, a group of college students took your case on. *Your case.* One out of hundreds to choose from. You don't think the Lord had anything to do with it?"

He'd never thought about it that way. "Well…"

Becoming more animated, Nate continued. "In addition, they worked hard and the professor oversaw it and made sure that the prosecutor listened. And the prosecutor actually did listen! Right?"

"Right."

Nate threw his hands up in the air. "Do you think that was just happenstance?"

He'd been so intent on wrapping himself in his bitterness, he'd never thought about things the way Nate had just laid it out. In a lot of ways, he felt stunned. "I don't know."

"Did you really not ask anyone to see how many cases there are in the Innocent Project?" When Daniel shook his head, Nate continued. "There's a whole bunch of them. Now, some of the men and women who claim to be innocent are probably guilty. But the court system is made of humans who are subjective and fallible. Mistakes happen."

"So you're saying me standing here is because of God intervening." Daniel realized he sounded skeptical and maybe even like a disbeliever, but he couldn't help it.

"I'm saying that He didn't let you down. Not this time. Not ever."

Daniel stared hard at him. As the seconds passed, he realized that Nate meant every word of what he'd said. Though he still wasn't completely sure that he trusted Nate a hundred percent, he was starting to believe that he needed to start believing in someone.

And, perhaps, rethink his feelings about God.

"What do you need from me?" he asked at last.

"I want to hear about that night again."

"Why? I know it's been already written down in the detective's notes or in the court transcripts."

"I have read that account but I still want to hear your version with my own ears."

"My version? Nate, I'm telling ya, everything I said was the truth. One minute I was standing with a crowd of people, the next, the lights went out, shots were fired and everyone started screaming and running. When I realized Brandt had been shot, I knelt by his side and tried to help him. That's when the cops came."

"I want to hear you tell me everything you remember about that night."

"I don't have a choice, do I?" He didn't even try to keep the bitterness out of his voice.

"Of course you have a choice. You are innocent. You've received restitution. You're not going to get in trouble or arrested."

"So I can refuse."

"You can, but I hope you won't. I wouldn't be here if I didn't think you could help me, Daniel."

"Fine. I will talk about it again, but not now and not here."

Nate stared at him intently. "It needs to be soon. I don't have months to make things right," he warned. "I have other cases on my docket."

"I know. I didn't ask for a month. Just one night. Give me until tomorrow. I'm tired and I'm standing in the front lawn of my brother's' house. You showing up caught me off guard. I'm kind of rattled. I've done my best to never think about that night."

Stuffing his hands in his pockets, Nate nodded. "All right. Fair enough. Tomorrow, then?"

Figuring that he might as well get it over with, Daniel nodded. "Yeah, sure. I have the day off. I can talk to you in the afternoon. I've got to go look at an apartment tomorrow. Since I have the day off, I'm gonna go in the morning."

"Are you going to move?"

"I hope so."

"It's not a done deal?"

"I only heard about it today."

"Ah. Good luck with that. So, where do you want to talk? Should I come back here?"

"No. How about at Jefferson Park? It's big and there are a lot of places to sit that are spread out."

"Sounds good." Heading to the door, he added, "I'll see you around two. That okay?"

"I'll be here."

Nate turned to meet his gaze. "Be safe, Daniel."

"What? Safe looking at a place to live?"

"No, kid. I'm talking about every hour of every day."

Daniel raised his eyebrows. "Because?"

"Have you seriously not connected the dots? Daniel, if you didn't kill Brandt then someone else did. And if the killer is still in the area, he'll know you're talking to me." He looked at him pointedly. "And telling me what you know. He might not like that."

"What, like I could be in danger?"

"All I'm saying is that you're not the only person who doesn't like going to prison. The real killer set you up. Now that you've been found innocent, word is going to get out that we've opened the case again."

Daniel felt his expression blanch, but he pulled himself together and walked through the door.

As he walked inside the dark house, he shivered. Like a ghost had just crossed his path. That had to be the reason there were now chill bumps on his arms.

Daniel had been rattled.

Nate was still thinking about Daniel's reaction to his warning when he stopped at BJ's Burgers on the edge of town. The small, old-fashioned-looking diner had been there for generations. Though he'd never gotten the chance to visit when he'd grown up nearby and was Amish, he had gotten the opportunity to visit several times over the last five years.

BJ's was known for their burgers, of course, but also for their shakes and malts. And daily specials that ran the gamut from turkey platters to spinach quiche to Salisbury steak.

Deciding to take a short break and eat an early dinner, he parked off to the side, pleased that it wasn't crowded, and entered.

A tall, slim woman was behind the center counter. "Hey!" she said with a smile. "How many?"

"One."

"Well, come on in, then. There's space at the bar."

There were eight spots and only one was filled. The man who was sitting at the end was reading the paper and eating a burger. Nate took a seat at the other end. It wasn't an ideal spot because he wasn't facing the door, but he figured it didn't matter. He didn't expect to see anyone he knew or run into any trouble.

"Here's a menu. The special today is chicken à la king."

"Really? You serve chicken à la king in a burger joint?"

"We're more like a diner, actually." The woman darted a look toward the back. "No offense to BJ in the kitchen, but it's not my favorite dish. I wouldn't recommend it."

"Noted."

"What do you want to drink? Soda? Water? Shake?"

"I better stick with water."

"Good idea. Stay hydrated."

He couldn't help but watch her stop to check on the

guy at the other end of the bar, fill his coffee cup, then fill a glass with ice and water. She was probably close to his forty years, and her red hair was cut into some sort of short, messy style. He knew enough to realize that her hairstyle looked like she'd stepped out of the shower, finger combed it and was ready, but he knew few women were able to get away with that.

All he did know was that there was something about her that was fresh and vibrant.

"Do you know what you want yet?"

He was surprised to realize that he hadn't thought about much but her. "No, not yet."

"Take your time. I'm here for another three hours."

"Thanks. Hey, I'm sorry I didn't catch your name."

Her blue eyes lit up. "That's probably because I never gave it to you. My name is Mitzi."

"I don't know if I've ever met a Mitzi before."

"You probably haven't. It's unusual."

"Nothing wrong with that."

"I've always thought the same thing. Hey, what about you?"

"Me?" She'd lost him.

"What's your name?"

"Nate."

"That name isn't too common, either. At least not around these parts."

"I guess we were meant to meet each other, then."

She laughed. "You let me know when you're ready to order, all right, Nate?"

He nodded, thinking that he might have just met her but he already couldn't wait to see her again.

Preferably sometime very soon.

Chapter Six

Lela hated to admit it, but on some days, pet sitting wasn't all that fun of a job. Sometimes the animals were shy or sad because they missed their owners or tried to bite her. Sometimes the owners asked her to do unreasonable things or didn't remember to pay her.

And, every once in a while, she had to watch dogs that had no interest in being trained or listening to her. This was one of those days.

As she continued walking her charge down the path at Cooper's Park, Lela wished she was pulling the dog into his own house.

Instead, she had almost a whole mile to go before that could happen. If her arm survived the walk, that is.

"Brownie, halt!"

Unfortunately, the fifty-four-pound fur ball kept pulling on his leash. The squirrel he was chasing picked up another acorn as if to tease him.

"Whoof!"

Using all her might, Lela pulled hard on the leash. Brownie stopped at last.

Lela was so, so happy about that. Honestly, who- ever believed that Labradoodles were lovely dogs surely hadn't met Brownie. Brownie didn't listen, ate every- thing in sight and pulled on his leash like nobody's business.

At least he was cute, super affectionate and didn't bite. "I've had more troublesome charges, that is for sure," she murmured as she stopped for a breather. Bending down slightly, she looked at Brownie in the eyes. "Brownie, I am certain that you are a very good dog sometimes. How about you pull me less and coop- erate more? That would make us both happy."

When Brownie wagged his tail, she took that as a good sign. "I'm pleased you agree. Now, if you sit, I'll give you some water." She had a backpack with a water bottle and a collapsible dog bowl inside.

"Whoof!"

"Nee, hund. Sit."

The dog didn't look pleased but surprisingly did as she asked.

"Well, look at you. You do listen!" Pulling off her backpack, she opened the water bottle, poured a bit of water into the bowl and then set it in front of Brownie. When he eagerly started lapping it up, she smiled. *"Gut hund.* Good dog." When his tail wagged again, she helped herself to a healthy drink, as well.

"Sorry, but he doesn't seem all that good to me."

Startled, Lela choked just as she was swallowing. As she continued to cough, she wondered how Daniel had snuck up so quietly on not just her but Brownie, too. Weren't all dogs supposed to be better at guard- ing than that?

"You—" And…she started coughing again. Ugh! Would she ever catch her breath?

Next thing she knew, Daniel was patting her on the back. She supposed he thought he was helping, but it was obvious that he didn't aid coughing women often. His pats felt more like heavy thumps.

"I'm so sorry, Lela," Daniel said. "I should've waited to speak until you were done sipping water."

When she realized he was about to thump her back again, she at last found her voice. "Stop trying to help me."

He froze. "It's not helping?"

She turned to face Daniel. "*Nee*. Your pats are too heavy. I'm not a burly man, you know." Now that she'd caught her breath, she stood up a little straighter and attempted to look put-upon.

Though his hands were now safely by his sides, he had the audacity to look amused. "As a matter of fact, I have noticed that you are neither a man nor burly. Unfortunately I don't have a lot of experience comforting women in need. Next time I'll try a gentler touch. I do apologize if I hurt you."

Carefully pushing away all thoughts of Daniel touching her in a more caring manner, she cleared her throat. "I'm fine. Just, ah, be careful. It would be awful if you patted your baby that forcefully."

"Yes, it would. Hopefully I'll have learned to temper my pats by the time I sire a child."

He was now sounding very, *very* amused. Sire a child, indeed.

Well, Lela supposed she didn't blame him. She'd just

chastised him like a wayward child, all because she couldn't seem to swallow water properly.

Deciding it was past time to delve into safer territory, she looked down at Brownie. The dog was still sitting quietly, his head going between the two of them like he was watching a tennis match. Impressed with his good manners, she rubbed the top of his head. "Good boy, Brownie."

Daniel smiled at the dog, as well. "His name is Brownie?"

"*Jah*. Due to his brown color, I suppose."

"I reckon so." He grinned. Kneeling down on one knee, he held out a hand for the Labradoodle to sniff, then gently rubbed the dog's neck. "I stand corrected, Brownie. You are a *gut hund*, ain't so?"

Brownie gifted him with two tail thumps.

After petting him for another moment, he stood up. "Whose dog is this?"

"An *Englisher* family's. They live nearby. One day a week, both the husband and wife work outside the house. Brownie gets lonely, so I take him for a walk, attempt to train him a bit and give him some attention."

"He's one blessed dog."

"Indeed. He's spoiled, for sure and for certain." She smiled at Daniel. "I can't say that I think that's a bad thing, though. He might not be too smart, and he pulls on my arm too much when we're walking, but he is a sweetheart."

"How much longer will you be watching him today?"

"Not long. We were heading back to his house when I decided to stop for a drink of water."

"May I walk you back?"

"Why?"

"No particular reason. I mean, not beyond the fact that I have a day off and have too much time on my hands."

Lela noticed that his expression had turned solemn. He really was in need of company. "You may walk with me, but you canna come inside Brownie's house."

"I wouldn't dream of it."

"Daniel, the things you say! Come on, then. Brownie, let's go home."

Unfortunately, that had been the wrong thing to say to the Labradoodle. The dog sprang to his feet and pulled on his leash.

And…there went her arm again. "Heel, Brownie."

He didn't listen, of course. He was practically wiggling, he was so excited to head back to his house.

"Brownie, *nee!*"

"Here. Let me help," Daniel said. He reached for the leash.

On another day, she wouldn't have given it up. Walking dogs was her job, after all. But her arm was tired. To her dismay, when Brownie pulled on his leash again, Daniel clicked his tongue. "*Nee*, Brownie," he said in a hard, certain tone. "We walk together, *jah*?"

When Brownie pulled again, Daniel stopped. "*Nee.* You walk with me, *hund.*"

Brownie's big brown eyes darted from Lela to Daniel, then sighed.

"Let's walk now, Brownie."

And just like that, the silly Labradoodle began walking by Daniel's side.

"*Jah*, that's right," he murmured.

In spite of herself, Lela was impressed. "How did you know to do that? Do you have a dog at home?"

"Nee." Looking embarrassed, he said, "Mansfield has a program for inmates to learn how to train therapy dogs. Once it was looking like there was a good chance that I was innocent, the warden allowed me to participate."

"It's a shame that you had to wait so long. How come you didn't get to do the program when you first arrived?"

"I was sentenced to ten years for involuntary manslaughter, Lela. No one is going to put a convicted murderer with a puppy until everyone is sure that I would treat it well."

She was outraged on his behalf. "Of course you would treat a puppy well."

Still walking Brownie, Daniel threw her a sideways look. "Unfortunately, you were not in charge of inmates' programs, Lela."

"I'm really glad you were set free."

"Me, too." He sighed. "Now all I have to do is hope that the police don't change their minds about me."

She gaped at him. "What are you saying? Do you really think they could charge you again?"

"I don't want to believe that, but anything is possible."

"But…but I thought there was new evidence or something."

"There's DNA evidence that I didn't shoot the gun that killed your cousin, but I wouldn't put it past the police to charge me as an accessory or something."

She shook her head. "My Uncle Nate wouldn't do that. He's a good man." Sure, she didn't exactly know him, but she knew enough about him to believe that.

Daniel still didn't look like he completely believed that. "He wants me to recount everything again."

"Will you?"

"Yeah. I mean, it's not like I have a choice. He's a cop."

"Nate wanting to hear your story is a good, right? Or…do you not think that will help?"

"I don't know. But I see his point. There aren't a lot of witnesses for him to interview." Looking straight ahead, he said, "Plus, it's to my benefit to help as much as I can…no matter how uncomfortable being around a policeman makes me."

Lela supposed Daniel had a point. She liked Uncle Nate a lot, but then again, she'd only ever known him as the uncle who left and rarely returned. Daniel had likely gotten to know a far different side of policemen.

Realizing they were almost back to Brownie's home, she pointed to the gray house on the corner. "We're almost there."

"Ah. I'll walk you to the front door and then leave you alone." He sounded the same but she could have sworn that there was a touch of sadness in his eyes.

"You don't have to leave me alone, Daniel. I mean, today, yes, but not always. I want to be your friend."

"I'd like us to be friends, too. Maybe next time I have a day off, I'll see you walking and we can chat again."

Lela knew what he was doing. Giving her space and allowing her to keep their relationship hidden from her parents. She appreciated his effort, but she didn't want to leave their next meeting completely to chance. "Are you working on Saturday?"

"Nee."

"If you don't have plans, would you like to meet me at the farmers market?"

"In the town square?" When she nodded, he added, "People will see us together."

"I know, but all they'll know is that we both just happened to be at the market. There's nothing wrong with that."

He studied her for a moment, then nodded. "I'll see you at the market, then. I reckon I'll get there around nine."

She smiled as they stopped in front of Brownie's family's front door. "I reckon I'll be there about the same time." She held out her hand. "Thank you for helping me with this silly dog."

"It was no problem. I enjoyed it." Bending down, he gently ran a hand along the dog's spine. "*Gut hund*, Brownie."

When he straightened, he handed her the leash. His fingers brushed against hers, lighting that same awareness between them that she seemed incapable of turning off. Her mouth went dry.

Tipping his hat, he murmured, "Good day, Lela. I'll see you on Saturday morning."

"Good day to you, too, Daniel."

With another small smile, Daniel Darrel Miller turned away. Unable to help herself, she watched him walk down the driveway then turn back the way they'd come.

Pulling out the house key from her backpack, she looked down at Brownie. "What do you think, Brownie? There's something there, don't you think?"

Unfortunately, all the dog seemed to care about was

entering his home—and receiving the dog treat she always gave him before she left his house for the day.

Ah, well. Lela supposed she couldn't blame Brownie. Everyone and everything had priorities. Her friendship with Daniel lagged far behind his comfy dog bed and a treat.

"Let's get you settled, Brownie," she said as she opened the door. "I think we've done enough for one day."

Brownie's happy bark conveyed he completely agreed.

Chapter Seven

The first time Daniel visited Jefferson Park was his first day of *rumspringa*. The park was a ways off— at least a good thirty-minute bike ride. That distance had made the rather run-down area seem more special than it actually was. He hadn't cared, though. All that mattered to him was that he was finally going to get to go to the place where all the older kids gathered from time to time.

Minutes before he'd left, his stomach a ball of nerves and excitement, his older brother, Abram, had given him all sorts of warnings about being careful. He'd even cautioned that there was no real reason to even have a run-around time. Some teenagers never did. Abram sure hadn't.

Daniel had ignored every well-intentioned bit of advice.

Of course, he hadn't imagined that he would get in any sort of trouble at all. He'd only thought he'd play ball with his friends, talk to some older teens and maybe see a girl or two. Well, all that, and the fact that he didn't have to be home until midnight. He'd felt so grown up.

Actually, nothing out of the ordinary had happened. He'd played basketball, flirted with Emma Hostetler and then gone out for ice cream. When he'd come home at ten that night, Abram had teased him bad.

"You and your big plans," he'd teased from his twin bed on the other side of the bedroom they shared. "See, I told ya that there was nothing special about *rumspringa*."

Daniel had gone to bed thinking that maybe his brother had been right.

The next time he'd visited the park had been a different story, though. Emma hadn't been there, no one wanted to play basketball and Wyatt had shown up just as Daniel had been about to head home at nine o'clock.

His first impression of Wyatt Troyer had been that Wyatt had seemed older than he'd stated. There had also been something a little off about him, too. Some of his Pennsylvania Dutch words weren't quite right, and his eyes were constantly darting around the area.

But Daniel soon ignored his misgivings because Wyatt had acted like he was something special. That had been new for him. He'd lived his life feeling like he was firmly in the middle. He wasn't all that strong or smart or handsome. He wasn't weak or dumb or ugly, either. He just was himself.

Except in Wyatt's light brown eyes.

Within just a few minutes of conversation, Wyatt had tapped into a need Daniel hadn't even realized he'd had. Next thing Daniel knew, he couldn't care less about

Emma or playing ball. He wanted to be around Wyatt, and Wyatt had seemed really pleased about that, too.

And then, of course, everything had gotten very bad, very fast.

Sitting on the park bench while he waited for Nate, Daniel wondered why he'd suggested Jefferson Park in the first place. Had he felt the need for Nate to actually see where his friendship with Wyatt had all started? Or, was revisiting this place more for him? Had he needed to see it six years later with a clear perspective?

"Sorry I'm late," Nate called out as he strode forward. Like Wyatt used to do, the detective was scanning the area as he approached. "Any special reason you chose this place to meet?"

"There is. It's where I first met Wyatt."

Taking a seat next to him, Nate pulled out a small tape recorder. "Do you mind if I record our conversation?"

"Nee."

After Nate spoke into the microphone, then played it back to test it, he pushed play again. "Tell me about that first visit."

Daniel did. He told Nate about how his brother had warned him that *rumspringa* was usually nothing special and how he'd been feeling a little let down that the big event he'd been looking forward to had been anticlimactic. And then he told Nate about his first impression of Wyatt.

"Tell me again what he looked like."

"Short red hair, scruff on his cheeks like he'd needed to shave. Lanky. A little bit shorter than I am now. I'm guessing maybe a few inches shy of six feet?"

"After you started talking, what happened? Did you make plans to meet again? Did he give you his phone number?"

Daniel shook his head. "*Nee*. He ended it with something like, 'I hope I'll see you around sometime.'"

Nate looked at him closely. "I'm guessing you did?"

"*Jah*. He…he drove up in his car on my way to work."

"What were you doing, Daniel?"

"I'd gotten a job at a lumber mill. They promised to train me, but I wasn't doing anything but cleaning and sweeping." Remembering how full of himself he'd been, he added, "I was sure they'd lied about an eventual apprenticeship and was sure they were only using me for cheap labor."

"You really didn't like sweeping floors, huh?"

"Not at all. I convinced myself that I was better than that."

"So, he drove up and what? Rolled down the window?"

Daniel nodded. "Yes. We talked. He asked if I wanted to go for a ride instead of working but I said no."

"How come?"

"I was too afraid I'd get in trouble." He sighed. "But the next time Wyatt drove up, I was in a real bad mood. I'd made the mistake of telling my brother that I was thinking of quitting and he'd told me that I was stupid for even thinking about quitting such a good job. So, when Wyatt asked if I wanted to take a break from my life, I took him up on his offer."

"What did you two do?"

"We came back here for a spell, but there were a lot of mothers and toddlers here, so Wyatt drove us out to an old barn he said was his grandfather's." Remembering how it looked old from the outside but far more secure inside, Daniel said, "I should have known right then that Wyatt wasn't Amish. The inside had a strand of lights attached to the rafters. There was also a cooler and a bunch of large wooden crates that had locks on them."

"What was inside?"

"I don't know. When we got there, Wyatt asked me if I wanted a beer. I couldn't think of an easy way to say I didn't, so I drank beer with him and he told me stories about some of the things he'd done."

"Such as?" Nate asked.

As the interview continued, Daniel told Nate about other visits, the alcohol. The pot. The pills that Wyatt had offered but he'd never accepted. Wyatt's hints about making money other ways. His stories about how much people would pay for some of their vices.

Though Daniel had told Detective Peck some of this information, the officer had seemed bored. Daniel's public defender hadn't cared about what he and Wyatt had done together, either. All he had done was say that he was going to try to get Daniel ten years or less. Daniel had been too scared to argue about that.

Nate turned off the recorder. "We've been talking for an hour. Do you need a break?"

"No. I'd rather just get this over with."

When he clicked back on the device, he said, "Tell me about the night of the party."

"It was at an apartment in Cleveland. I'd ridden there with Wyatt, a friend of his who was older than him, two girls Wyatt knew and Brandt. None of them paid much attention to me or Brandt."

"Because you were so much younger?"

"Yeah. And because Brandt looked scared to death. I'd been so eager to have someone else from my community doing the same things I was, I'd practically forced Brandt to come to the party with me."

"So he was scared?"

"Yeah. The minute we got there, I knew I shouldn't have brought him." Remembering how Brandt had kept looking at him like he was a stranger, Daniel felt tears threaten.

"What happened when you got to the apartment?"

"It was dark outside. Probably eight or nine at night. When we arrived, the party was in full swing. There must have been forty people there. Wyatt went off with that guy, and the girls walked away to be with some of their friends or something."

"Was everyone Amish?"

"It was hard to tell, but I knew at least some of them were. Like me and Brandt, they were wearing *Englisher* clothes that were either brand new and cheap, or clothes that they'd already borrowed from other kids." With a sigh, he continued. "Brandt and I got beer and then someone brought in a bunch of pizzas, and everyone started eating. Wyatt pulled me away to meet some people." Forcing himself to add more, Daniel said, "Wyatt asked me to start selling for him. This time, instead of shaking my head no, I told him I'd think about it."

"Why?"

"I needed money. I'd been let go from the lumber yard and my whole family was angry with me. All I could think about was getting out on my own. I needed money to do that."

"I see." Nate looked at him intently. "Did Brandt overhear you agree to dealing?"

"I don't think so...but maybe?" Realizing that he'd never considered that his buddy might have overheard, Daniel felt sick. "I lost track of Brandt, though I did see him talking to Wyatt privately for a while."

"Any idea what they were talking about?"

He started to shake his head then remembered that Brandt had appeared to be lecturing Wyatt. "If I had to guess, it was that Wyatt was feeling Brandt out to see what he thought about dealing and got an earful. No way would Brandt have been okay with that."

"And then?"

Steeling himself for the worst part, he said, "Then the lights went out. I don't know if a circuit was blown or someone did it on purpose, but it was pitch-black. People started shining their phones around. The party got crazier. Then the older guy who had ridden with us pulled out a gun. A couple of people wanted to get their picture taken with it. Eventually the gun was passed to me."

Nate leaned forward. "You took the weapon?"

Daniel nodded. "Yeah. I didn't take my picture or anything, but I wasn't afraid of it. I just held the gun for a second before I passed it on to the next person."

"Where was Brandt? Was he back by your side?"

"*Nee.*" Remembering the way Brandt had looked at him, Daniel felt a lump form in his throat. "Brandt was standing across the room. If I had to guess, he was trying to think of a way to leave."

"And then?"

"And then next thing I knew, a couple of guys started fighting. A couple of minutes later, a few more guys joined in. People were either egging them on or getting out of the way, then someone fired the gun up in the air." Remembering the chaos, the confusion, the darkness...and how it was all mixed up in a drunken haze, he added, "I thought someone fired it to try to stop the fight."

"What happened? Did the fight stop?"

"I don't know if the shots did that, or the girl that started screaming." Hating the memories, he swallowed hard. "When a light came on at last, Brandt was on the ground, bleeding something awful. I was sure that someone shot him on accident."

"Maybe that is what happened...or maybe it wasn't."

"Or maybe not, I don't know. All I do know is that everyone scattered, the cops came fast, and they found me sitting on the ground next to Brandt, who was dead. Nearby was the gun."

Nate turned off the recorder. "Okay. I think I have a better idea of what happened."

Daniel wasn't sure what the cop had gleaned but he was too worn-out by the memories to care. "Can I leave now?"

"Are you okay?"

"Yeah. I... It doesn't matter how long it's been or how many times I've given myself excuses, it's still hard to realize that I'm responsible for Brandt's death. If I hadn't brought him to that party, he would still be alive."

Nate shook his head. "You might be guilty of being naive or stupid, but you didn't shoot the gun, Daniel.

You didn't know that was going to happen. You are innocent." Looking at him intently, Nate added, "Actually, I'd say you are as much of a victim as Brandt."

"I know you told me that before, but I don't know. I do know that by the time the cops came, most everyone else was gone."

"Wyatt didn't wait for you?"

"No. He ran. Most of the guys ran. I think someone set me up."

Nate stared at him intently. "Have you ever thought that maybe Brandt's death wasn't a random thing? Maybe someone killed him on purpose and set you up to take the fall."

"Then that means that there's a reason someone at that party wanted Brandt to die."

"What do you think?"

Daniel realized that he wasn't shocked by the theory. Actually, in some of his darkest moments in prison, he had considered that his friend's death wasn't completely random. He'd just been so consumed by guilt, he hadn't wanted to believe in the possibility. "I think that might be true," he said.

Nate nodded. "All right, then. I'm going to start digging even harder."

"If you need my help, you have it."

"Thanks. I appreciate that. We're going to get that guy. I promise."

Daniel wanted to believe the detective. He really did. But Brandt was dead and was never going to be able to share his part of the story. Figuring out what really happened—and why—seemed as far-fetched as going back in time.

But revealing that wouldn't be right. So he merely stood up and shook Nate's hand. "Thank you for wanting to hear my whole story. No one ever wanted to hear it before."

"I wish they would've. I really do."

As Daniel walked home, he tried to think about the garage apartment he was going to move into. Tried to think about his job. About Lela.

But the only thing that came to his mind was the way Brandt had looked when he'd been bleeding on the floor.

Chapter Eight

Kelley's Farmers Market was more crowded than usual. Well, at least it seemed that way to Daniel. It had been a very long time since he'd gone on a Saturday. Years before he'd gone to prison.

The thought shamed him.

When Daniel was still in his teens, his mother had asked him to accompany her. She asked all three of them. But while Abram and Violet had often accompanied her, he had only done so after complaining loudly. He'd thought spending a few hours helping his mother carry bags of fruits and vegetables was a waste of time, though what he'd thought he was so busy doing, he had no idea.

Back then, before he'd met Wyatt, he'd been just a stupid kid with big dreams of the outside world and moving far away. The irony of what had happened was not lost on him. During the trial, he'd ached for things to go back to the way they were. That was when he'd learned that saying something as simple as "I'm sorry" both meant the world and was a useless expression all at the same time. It might make the person you harmed feel better, but in the end, it didn't change the past.

"Daniel, you made it!"

"*Jah*, Bishop Schlabach, I did." He and the bishop had run into each other at the store, and the man had chastised him for buying apples there. He'd practically made Daniel promise to visit the farmers market on Saturday.

Looking mighty pleased, the gray-haired man patted his shoulder. "I'm glad, son. You're going to have a grand time." Just as Daniel was about to reply, the other man frowned. "Wait, where's your tote?"

"My tote?" He had no idea what the bishop was talking about.

"For all the items you'll be purchasing." He continued on in a rush. "Oh, I know. You're likely thinking about the way things used to be. We've become more environmentally responsible now, *jah*?"

"I didn't know that." He'd also never expected to hear such a phrase from the man.

"Oh. Well, we used to be able to get plastic bags from the vendors, but that hurts the landfills, ain't so? No worries," he continued. "I have three bags with me today. I'll be happy to share." He handed him a green bag with the words Mammoth Cave on the side.

Daniel wasn't all that sure he wanted to carry a tote at all, but it was in his hands before he had come up with a reason to refuse. "Are you sure you won't need it, Bishop?"

"I'm sure. You enjoy yourself, son. I'm glad you're here." A twinkle entered his eyes. "I have a feeling that someone else is gonna be real glad you're here, as well."

Daniel stared at the bishop's retreating form with a sense of dismay, then decided that he might as well go shopping. He did need more apples, after all.

Just as he turned, he saw Lela. When she met his gaze, he smiled and immediately felt his neck heat up. He mentally berated himself. Why, why did he always act like a shy, awkward teen whenever he was around her?

When he didn't smile in return, she quickly looked down at her feet and then turned away.

And...now he'd embarrassed her.

You've got to get it together, he told himself. Figuring he needed all the help he could get, he reached out to the only one who could make things easier. *God, I could use a little bit of help right now.*

Just as Lela darted behind a group of *Englishers*, he finally got his feet to move. Crunching up the green tote in his hand, he weaved through the crowd, scanning every group of people standing together. Looking for some sign of Lela and her bright blue dress.

The farmers market turned around a corner. A trio of teenagers were playing guitars and singing some sort of folk song. They'd drawn quite a crowd.

Quickly as he could, Daniel stepped around them, and finally caught sight of her in the distance speaking to Ada Walker.

Daniel frowned. It wasn't that he didn't like Ada, it was that she was a shameless busybody. Well, if facing Ada and her too-perceptive gaze was what he was going to have to do, then he'd do it. Whatever it took to make things right with Lela.

Just as Daniel was about to increase his stride, a

mother pushing a stroller and a grumpy toddler stepped in front of him. He abruptly stopped just as the tot yelled "No!" and pulled away from his *mamm*.

To his dismay, the boy charged right into his knees.

The toddler might be little, but he'd hit Daniel with enough force that he'd let out a lungful of air. "Umph!"

The contact startled the child enough to stare at Daniel with wide eyes.

Daniel knelt down to steady him. "You all right?" he asked.

The little boy nodded.

"I'm so sorry!" the mother said. "Peter, you are being naughty. Tell that man you are sorry."

Still staring at Daniel, he did as bid. "Sorry."

"It's all right. But mind your *mamm*, *jah*? She only wants to keep you safe."

The mother, obviously hearing his words, smiled. "Thank you. Peter, come along and we'll go get some cucumbers"

Crisis obviously forgotten, Peter smiled at him as they went on their way.

Getting to his feet, Daniel looked back to where Lela had been standing. Only Ada was there, unabashedly watching him. He'd lost Lela.

Walking toward Ada, he scanned the area again. And then felt something akin to a bolt of lightning hit his heart. There, in the crowd, also staring at him, was Wyatt.

Wyatt, who'd befriended him and happily led him astray.

Wyatt, who'd given him liquor and sold him drugs.

Wyatt, who had encouraged him to take Brandt to the party in Cleveland.

Wyatt, who the police had said never existed.

Daniel blinked, sure his eyes were deceiving him. Maybe his imagination had taken flight and he was seeing things.

But no, it was Wyatt Troyer, all right. There, standing bold as brass in the middle of his town was the man who'd haunted his dreams. He had the same red hair, same scruffy cheeks, same slightly bloodshot, light brown eyes. The only difference was that his thin frame seemed to be even thinner. He was bordering on gaunt.

Everything inside of Daniel wanted to march over and speak to Wyatt and give him a piece of his mind. No, yell at him. Berate him for everything he'd done. For everything he'd caused. For turning Daniel into a fugitive in his own hometown.

He clenched his hands as his pulse quickened and the anger threatened to consume him.

He stepped forward, then looked down at his hands. They were in tight fists. His body was preparing to hit Wyatt.

He knew he could take him down easily, too. Daniel worked hard at Carter and Sons. His body had filled out from a healthy diet of fresh, hearty food and all of the physical labor he did.

In addition, he surely knew how to fight now. He'd learned the first week in prison the consequences of not standing up for himself. At least once a week he'd fought someone.

Wyatt would be no match for him.

Daniel's mouth went dry as every dark part of his

brain pushed him forward. He wanted vengeance. He needed to do something to hurt Wyatt.

Vengeance is mine.

He drew to a stop, stung by the Lord's admonishment. Right then and there he knew that his savior knew better and was providing him a better way to live.

He might have been in prison, but he wasn't there any longer.

He might have needed Wyatt to confess to shooting Brandt, but it wouldn't change anything.

The Lord had already taken care of Daniel. He'd gotten him out of prison and helped him in so many ways since he'd returned.

There was only one thing to do.

He walked away.

Daniel had thought the move would be physically painful but it wasn't. It wasn't at all.

Because the moment he turned away and started back the way he came, he saw Lela again. His reward.

"Daniel, hiya!" she called out with a bright smile. "Come look what I just bought."

Giving thanks again, he headed toward her. Both his step and his soul feeling lighter.

Chapter Nine

Daniel was actually heading her way. And, wonder of wonders, he was even kind of smiling. Lela could hardly believe it, though why that was, she didn't know. After all, she'd surely made a cake of herself, calling out to him in the middle of the market. At least twenty people had stopped what they were doing and stared. Daniel really hadn't much choice but walk over to her.

No doubt at least a few of the people watching would gossip about who she was talking to. Someone would probably tell her mother.

Who would, of course, sit Lela down and give her a stern talking to.

Lela didn't care, though. All she did care about was that handsome, mesmerizing Daniel Miller was heading her way.

When Daniel drew to a stop in front of her, he folded his hands behind his back. "Hiya, Lela."

She couldn't resist smiling. "Daniel."

"I'm glad to see you."

"I'm glad to see you, too." She beamed at him.

When he grinned again, she felt a little foolish. He was older and far more worldly than she. No doubt she was coming across even more naive than ever.

But if she didn't stop gazing at him and say something quickly, he was going to walk away and think she was even more flighty than he probably already thought. Desperate for something to talk about, she dug into her canvas shopping bag and pulled out a gourd.

"Daniel, look what I just found. It's a gourd in the shape of a dog."

A gourd? A dog-shaped gourd was the best she could do?

Mentally, she slapped her forehead in aggravation. She wouldn't have thought it possible, but she'd just managed to sound even more foolish.

If he was taken aback, he covered up the reaction quickly. "A gourd, hmm?"

Since she couldn't really do anything but embrace her words, she smiled. *"Jah."*

"Let me see." To his credit, he didn't sound sarcastic at all. Instead, his tone was almost gentle.

"Here you go. What do you think?"

After she handed it to him, he rested the thing on the center of his palm. "Well...ah."

This was beyond embarrassing. "You have it upside down, silly." Leaning close, she turned the gourd right side up. "Do ya see the *hund* now?"

Daniel tilted his head to one side. "Kind of."

"Daniel, let your eyes relax and imagine what it could be."

It was obvious that he was trying not to grin. "You

want me to imagine that it's something beyond a simple gourd?"

Yes, she sounded like an idiot. But it was too late to go back, anyway. In for a penny, in for a pound. Stepping even closer, she ran a finger along the top of it. "See? This here is the back, and this is the head. And these bumps look a bit like ears, right?" She lifted her chin. "Do you see now?"

But he wasn't looking at the gourd at all. Instead, he was staring at her intently. Like everything she said mattered to him. Like he didn't think she was too immature for him at all.

And then, like the idiot she was, she couldn't do anything but stare back at him. Notice that his hazel eyes had flecks of gold in them. That his cheeks were dusted with a fine sprinkling of stubble. That his bottom lip was lightly chapped, as if he bit on it a little too often.

She was tempted to run a finger along that lip. Just to ease his skin.

Just to…

She inhaled sharply, shocked at the direction her mind was heading. "Oh!" She stepped backward.

Of *course* she took too big of a step and knocked into a shopper making his way behind her.

She turned. "I'm sorry!"

"It's okay, honey. Be careful now, right?" the man replied.

As she turned around, she glanced at Daniel again. "It's okay if you don't see the shape of a dog. I don't know what I was thinking."

"*Nee*, I see it." Though the rest of him looked as solemn as ever, his eyes were sparkling.

"How about I put this away and we try to forget I ever mentioned a gourd?" Just as she reached out to take the item out of his hand, a rush of people surged by. Next thing she knew, Daniel was shoved hard.

It made him lose his footing, and then lose his balance. He took a step toward her, but it was too short, and a child ran by, causing him to trip.

And down he went. He landed on one knee with so much force she was sure she heard a pop.

"Daniel!" She started to crouch down to help him.

"*Nee*, Lela. Stay there," he barked.

She did as he asked as he pushed himself to his feet. Only then did she notice that his hands were bloody.

"You're bleeding!"

He looked down at his palms and frowned. "It seems I am."

She reached for his arm. "Come with me and we'll sit down. I bet I can get someone in one of these booths to give us some paper towels or something."

But before she could make contact, he pulled his hand away. "Don't touch me."

His voice was so harsh, almost as if he'd thought she'd hurt him or something. "But I only want to help, *jah*? Please, let me—"

"Lela, I am bleeding."

Again, his rough tone of voice caught her off guard. "*Jah*. That's why I'm concerned, right?" When he still was avoiding her touch, she chuckled. "Daniel, I promise that I've seen blood before. I'm not squeamish."

It still felt wrong. Even though he knew it wasn't true, he felt like even his blood was tainted. "I don't want the blood to stain your dress."

She shook her head. Instead of searching for a paper towel, she pulled a clean handkerchief out of a pocket in her dress and pressed it to his palm. Immediately a red spot stained the starched cloth.

It was ruined.

Feeling like the cloth was a symbol for their relationship, he turned and walked away. His gait was painful, he was limping so badly.

Seeing that he'd left his tote bag on the ground, she bent down to pick it up. For a moment she was tempted to take it to him, but she decided against it.

She had a feeling he wouldn't thank her for chasing after him.

And maybe, if their positions were reversed, she would feel the same way.

After all, she'd embarrassed him.

Or maybe he didn't like that she'd witnessed his embarrassment, though he really had nothing to be embarrassed about. The crowd that had passed behind him had been unruly, and the child nearby had prevented him from moving.

Then a flash of something caught her mind. No, it hadn't been just the crowd. It had been a push. A man in a green shirt had pushed Daniel. She was sure of it.

But he was Amish and a stranger. Why would someone do something like that on purpose? It didn't make sense.

Hating the direction of her thoughts, she pushed them aside. Having such dark thoughts was wrong. She should be ashamed of herself.

Chapter Ten

Most days, Daniel was at peace with his decision to get baptized and wholeheartedly embrace Amish living. He believed in the teachings that his parents and grandparents had taught him. He found comfort in the peace and orderliness of his life. He appreciated doing without the many distractions that pulled his attention away from the things that really mattered—the people he was with and his relationship with the Lord.

Unfortunately, today wasn't one of those days. If he wasn't living Amish, he would've hopped in his car and gone to the doctor. Instead, he was attempting to make do.

Of course, there were many in the Amish community who would have reminded him that living Amish did not mean staying away from common sense and hospitals. They would be right. He didn't want to make a fuss, though.

But his resolution wasn't going very well. His knee was swollen to double its normal size and pained him considerably. And his palms, though they were only

scratched and cut, made it difficult to do even the simplest of things.

Even his job, it seemed.

When he spied his boss heading his way, he put down
his hammer and turned to face him. "Do you need something, Craig?"

"You could say that. Grab your tool belt and come
with me. You won't be coming back here today."

He was getting fired. Stark fear enveloped him as he
thought about the ramifications. He wouldn't be able
to stay in Abraham's cozy apartment. He'd have to go
farther to find a decent job because no one else in Lodi
would likely hire him.

Although that wasn't Craig's problem.

After carefully inserting the hammer into its leather
casing, he nodded. "There's no need to escort me out. I
can leave on my own."

Craig's eyebrows rose. "Daniel, do you think I'm
firing you?"

Why did his boss look so surprised? "Well, *jah*. I
mean, aren't ya?"

"I told ya that he'd think the worst," Abraham called
out from his perch at the top of a ladder.

Becoming even more confused, Daniel turned back
to face Craig. "What's going on?"

"I'm taking you to my doctor, that's what."

"Why?"

"Don't play dumb, kid. Your hands are cut to shreds
and it's obvious that your knee is swollen up like a balloon. You need to get checked out by someone who
knows what he's doing."

Though his body was practically cheering at the

thought of getting some relief, he shook his head. "I'm fine. I'll be better tomorrow."

"Doubt it. Stop being so stubborn and come with me."

It seemed he was going to have to be completely honest. "I can't afford a doctor's visit right now," he said. It was embarrassing but the truth.

Craig's expression was full of compassion. "I know, son. That's why I'm taking you to my doctor and not the hospital. Dr. Jackson is terrific and doesn't charge a fortune for his services."

That sounded good. But, did he really want to take up so much of his boss's time? No, he did not. "Thanks, but I'm sure I'll be all right in a day or two."

Craig folded his arms over his chest. "I've already called, and he can see you in thirty minutes. Come on. We don't want to be late. He's one of the few docs who runs on time."

Feeling the other men's gazes resting on him, Daniel followed Craig out the door and into his large black truck. After he turned onto the highway, Daniel said, "How did you know I needed to be seen? Was it really that obvious?"

"Kid, your hands are full of bandages and you can hardly walk. It was more than obvious that something was going on."

"I guess that's true."

"Then, there was the fact that Abraham clued me in about what happened at the farmers market on Saturday. What a crazy thing to happen. I'm sorry about that."

"*Jah.* Me, too." However, the more he thought about it, the more he was sure that someone had pushed him on purpose. And not just "someone," either. He was almost a hundred percent certain that it had been Wyatt. He'd even used Abraham's phone shanty and left a message for Detective Borntrager. He had no idea if his story would be believed but he'd felt compelled to share it.

Craig rested his elbow on the driver's side window. "Daniel, since we're alone right now, I think we ought to talk about something."

"Okay…"

His jaw worked. "Kid, I've always thought you got a bum rap about that boy's murder. We didn't know each other, but I know enough people who do know of ya to realize that something had gone terribly wrong." He drew a breath. "Then, when everything came out with you being innocent and the detective on the case didn't really look at other suspects? Well, I thought that was a real shame."

He didn't know how to respond so he simply nodded.

After glancing at him again, Craig continued. "All this means that I'm on your side, kid. I'm not going to fire you because you got knocked down and hurt your knee and hands in the middle of a farmers market."

"I wouldn't blame you if you did."

"I get where you are coming from, but I want you to start trying to believe in me. I'm not out to 'catch' you being bad or want to look for ways that you aren't working hard. I want you to be happy working for Carter and Sons. Do you understand?"

"Yes."

"Good. Accidents happen, and it says a lot that even though you were in pain you still came to work. I appre-

ciate that, but you also need to be honest with me—and
Zeke and the other guys you work with. If you aren't
your best, then it could affect not only the work you're
doing but everyone else's safety."

"I hadn't thought about it that way but I should have.
Thanks."

He waved a hand. "No reason to thank me for caring. Right?"

Craig sounded so grumpy and out of sorts, Daniel
almost smiled. "Right."

"Good. I'm real glad we got that straightened out."

"Me, too."

In no time at all they were at the doctor's office. Unlike the modern office Daniel had imagined, the office was in an old farmhouse. It was painted yellow
and had black shutters and two mums nestled in navy
blue pots on either side of the door. The bright, sunny
decor reminded him of Lela. There was a happiness
about both of them.

"This looks different than I imagined," he said as
they approached the door.

"It's nice, right? Mrs. Jackson is the office manager
and chief decorator. At least, that's what Dr. Jackson
always says. I think she does a good job."

"Me, too."

The door opened into a rather small waiting area.
There were only six chairs against the wall. Across
from the chairs were a small table and pair of chairs
with an abacus or some such on it. At one end of the
room were a large counter and space that led back to
the examining rooms.

No other patients were in the room. A middle-aged

African American woman smiled at them on the other side of the counter. "Craig, you're here right on time."

He held up a watch-covered wrist. "I'm seven minutes early, Mrs. Jackson. You know I wouldn't be late."

She laughed. "You're a charmer, that's what you are." Looking his way, she softened her tone. "You must be Daniel."

"Yes."

"Can you read and write English?"

"I can."

"Great. Come fill out the form for me. Anything you don't know the answer to, leave blank. My husband would rather have questions to ask instead of a bunch of lies he's trying to sort through."

"I understand."

"Good." She handed him the form and he sat down to fill it out.

Less than ten minutes later he was sitting in the examining room and Dr. Jackson was carefully manipulating his leg. "When did this happen again?"

"Saturday."

"You've been walking around and working all this time?"

Daniel nodded.

"Are you in a lot of pain?"

He considered lying but decided there was no point in that. "Yes."

"I'd be shocked if you weren't. Sorry, son, but we're going to need some X-rays."

"Where do I get those?"

"Here." He smiled. "We added an X-ray machine three years ago. It's been a real blessing for all of our patients. It's not the fanciest one around but it does the trick." He patted Daniel's shoulder. "And don't worry. If the films aren't as clear as we need them to be, I'll send you to the hospital for a CT scan or another set."

He could only imagine how much that would cost. "I hope we don't have to do that."

"Me, too, son. Now, let's deal with your hands. I need to clean them." The nurse had taken the bandages off when he'd first gotten into the examining room. "I'm going to call Kim in to help me. I've got to warn you that you're going to need a couple of shots in your palms, though. The shots will numb you up real well, but the needles don't feel too good going in."

"I don't need my palms to get numbed."

"Sorry, but I disagree." He pointed to a raised bump that had steadily gotten worse looking. "See that? You've got something stuck in your wound. Likely a piece of glass or a sliver of rock. Whatever it is, it needs to come out."

"Yes, sir."

"Ah, that's what I like to hear. A man unafraid to listen to me."

Daniel knew he was joking. He smiled sheepishly as Dr. Jackson called out for Kim and put on gloves. Moments later, the nurse was numbing his palms. He inhaled sharply when the needle poked.

Kim smiled at him in sympathy. "Sorry. I know this hurts."

"I'm fine." When she raised her eyebrows, Daniel decided that it was time—past time—to stop acting so stoic. "I mean, *jah*, it hurts, but I'm grateful to get the cuts cleaned out."

She chuckled. "You're something else, Daniel. Grateful, indeed."

An hour later, Craig was driving him back to his apartment. To Daniel's immense relief, his kneecap was bruised and battered but hadn't sustained anything too bad. The most surprising thing was how bad his palms had been.

"Stay home tomorrow. Abraham can tell me how you're doing when he gets to work. If you're feeling better, we'll put you back on the schedule for Friday."

"All right."

"I'm glad you don't have a broken kneecap, son."

"I am, too. Thank you for taking me."

"You're welcome." He parked in Daniel's drive. "Next time, ask for help."

"I will, though I really hope there isn't a next time."

"You and me both, son. See you in a few."

After Daniel let himself inside, he laid down on his bed. He hadn't taken a nap in ages, but today he wasn't going to fight it. He needed some rest. Nate was coming by that evening to talk about Daniel's sighting of Wyatt.

Daniel wanted to have his wits about him in case the detective was skeptical about his story.

Chapter Eleven

Nate had gotten back to Lodi too early to immediately head to Daniel's place. After much debate, he stopped by BJ's Burgers and went inside. Nowadays he tried not to eat too many burgers and fries, since his doctor hadn't been shy about his recent cholesterol levels. But BJ's served some really good ones, some of the best he'd ever had. And, if he was being honest, he was excited about the possibility of seeing Mitzi again. There was something about the woman, so comfortable in her long skirts, T-shirts and slip-on tennis shoes that got to him. Even though she was in her forties, he thought she was cute in that fresh-faced way one usually viewed younger women.

Whatever the reason, her pretty smile and easy manner felt like an oasis of calm in his turbulent life. There was a part of him that couldn't get enough of being around her. He hoped she was working.

The minute he walked through the door, he found himself scanning the restaurant for her. Then, there she was.

She'd just poured some coffee for a pair of men when he walked in. When she smiled, Nate let himself pretend that the smile was just for him.

"You're back!" she said.

She sounded so delighted—or maybe he was the one who felt that way—he couldn't resist chuckling. "Yeah. I guess I couldn't stay away."

After murmuring something to the men in the booth, she walked over to him. "The burgers really are to die for."

He knew the burgers had nothing to do with his return. "Don't say that," he joked. "My doc is going to give me a lecture if my cholesterol goes up."

Instead of scoffing, Mitzi looked thoughtful. "I have some ideas for that. Go sit down wherever and I'll be right over."

Nate wondered what was on her mind but just smiled in return as he walked to a table in the back corner.

"Here's a glass of water for you," Mitzi said. "And a menu."

"Thanks."

She opened it up and pointed to two burgers at the bottom of the menu. He hadn't noticed them the last time he was there. One was black bean and another was made of turkey. "You should get one of these and have a cup of vegetable soup as your side."

He couldn't help but wrinkle his nose. "I don't know."

"I promise, you'll like both. A lot of people order them. At least give one a try. And BJ's soup is really good."

"Let me think on it."

Tucking a wisp of her red hair behind an ear, she nodded. "All right."

She turned and headed back to the kitchen. Watching her walk away, Nate could've sworn she looked disappointed in him. He wondered why.

An elderly lady whom he hadn't noticed at first in the booth on the other side of the aisle chuckled. "Mitzi's got you thinking, doesn't she, young man?"

"Yes. And I'm not that young."

"That's true, but you still look all right."

"Thank you."

She sniffed. "You won't keep looking good if you don't start eating better, though. Mark my words."

What was going on? He was sitting in a diner that specialized in burgers, fries and shakes, but everyone seemed to act like it was the healthiest place in town. "Have you ever had the black bean burgers?"

"I have. The turkey ones, too, though I usually just have a salad and soup."

"And pie?" he couldn't help but refer to the plate on her table.

"Of course, pie, son. It's all choices, you know?"

"Yes." He'd just started reading the menu again when the diner's door opened and his niece entered. He stood up. "Lela."

A deer-in-the-headlights look appeared on her expression before it vanished. "Hi, Uncle Nate. How are you?"

"I'm fine. I came in for a quick bite to eat. Are you meeting someone here?"

"*Nee.* I'm alone."

"I'm alone, too. Would you like to join me?"

Her eyes widened again. He didn't need to wonder about why. Her parents practically thought of him as an enemy. He was tempted to give her an out, but then changed his mind. Lela wasn't a child, and he wanted to get to know her better. If nothing else happened during this investigation, at least he'd have that.

After the span of just a few seconds, she seemed to make up her mind and walked to his booth.

Sliding in the space across from him, she smiled. "I canna believe you're here."

"I'm glad I am. Seeing you is a nice surprise. It's the best part of my day."

As he'd hoped, Lela relaxed a bit. As much as he wanted to solve this case, he was coming to realize that he wanted to get to know his sweet niece better. At the very least, he wanted her to realize that she would always have a friend in him.

When Mitzi approached again, she was all smiles as she handed a glass of water and a menu to his niece. "Hi. Have you been here before?"

"Once, a long time ago."

"Well, we have all sorts of tasty things. I've been working here for years so I've tried just about everything. My favorites are the malts. I recommend the strawberry."

"Hey, how come my niece gets to hear about malts and I'm hearing about turkey burgers?"

One eyebrow arched. "You know why." Softening her voice, she said, "Do you want something else to drink besides water right now?"

"Um, a Coke?"

"Sure, honey. I'll be right back."

When they were alone again, Nate said, "What's new?"

She shrugged. "Everything. Nothing."

"That's intriguing."

"I was babysitting for most of today. Gwen came home a little early but insisted on paying me for the whole time, so I decided to take myself here."

"Is your mother going to get mad at you?"

"Probably. But nothing too bad. She won't tell my father or anything."

Nate hated that that was always a worry, but it didn't surprise him. Her father kept a tight rein on his family. He wasn't out of the norm, either. He'd seen enough to know that not every Amish family or community worked like that. As much as traditions, values and the *Ordnung* were respected, there was also a sense of understanding that the outside world wasn't miles away. For some Amish, the outside world was simply next door. The notion of never being around anything English was next to impossible.

By the time Mitzi arrived with Lela's soda, they were ready to order.

"What did you decide on?" she asked him, her pencil hovering over the pad of paper.

"The black bean burger and the soup."

Her eyes were fairly sparkling. "Good choice. And you, dear?"

"I was thinking maybe the chocolate shake?"

"The shakes are very good, too. Do you want anything to eat with that?"

Realizing that Lela was probably thinking about the cost, Nate said, "This is my treat, Lela. You want a burger or something, honey?"

She bit her lip, like there were too many choices. "Can…can I just have some French fries?"

"Of course. I'll get right on that."

As she walked away, Nate grinned at Lela. "Mitzi was just encouraging me to eat healthier when you arrived."

"Why was she doing that?"

"Because I happened to mention that my cholesterol was heading out of control."

"She's right, then. You do need to watch what you eat. You only have one body, you know."

It seemed everyone was full of good advice. "I know." Feeling sheepish, he said, "I need to go to more farmers markets and get some fresh vegetables and fruit."

"You should. I was just there on Saturday. There was a good selection and it all looked wonderful *gut*. All the fresh produce would encourage anyone to eat healthier."

Nate smiled at Lela's earnest expression. "I hear you loud and clear." Taking a chance, he added, "Did you happen see Daniel there?"

Instantly her guard went up. "Why are you asking about Daniel?"

Reminding himself that his niece was already a little tentative around him, he shrugged. "No reason. Daniel left me a message about his visit to the market on Saturday. I wondered if you happened to run into him."

She waited a second or so to answer. It was obvious that she was debating whether to divulge what was on her mind or not. Nate had witnessed this same hesitation over and over again during the course of his career. He'd learned staying silent got more answers than pressing for information.

He sipped his water and scanned the diner. Mitzi was chatting with a young couple. The man was holding a baby carrier, and all three of them were cooing at the babe nestled inside.

"As a matter of fact, I did see him."

"Oh?" He focused on her again.

Looking troubled, she added, "It was so crowded and some people were really rude. Someone knocked into Daniel and he fell."

"That's too bad."

"Jah." Her gaze darted around the restaurant before returning to him. "Uncle Nate, I thought I saw something, but I probably was mistaken."

Knowing that Daniel was sure it wasn't an accident, Nate was careful to phrase his question in the right way. "You saw something happen?"

She nodded. "Oh, *jah*." She looked about to add something but shook her head.

"What were you about to say?"

She sipped her water. "Nothing."

The skin prickled on the back of his neck. It might be his imagination, but he doubted it. So, even though he'd just told himself to tread lightly, he pushed a bit. "Lela, what do you think you saw?"

"I'm not really sure. I could've imagined it…"

"Lela, even if you were mistaken, I'd really like to know what you think you might have seen."

"Okay." She nibbled her bottom lip. "I thought I saw someone push Daniel."

Nate was pretty sure that his niece wouldn't make something like that up. "I see. Do you, ah, remember what this person looked like?"

She frowned. "Not really."

"Anything you can remember would be helpful. Was it a man or a woman?"

"A man," she replied. "Hey, why are you interested? It can't be important, can it? Surely knocking into someone isn't a crime."

"It isn't, but it could be a clue about the case that I'm working on. It might be. What do you remember?"

"Not much."

Deciding to push, he said, "Was this man Amish or English?"

She answered immediately. "Amish."

"Was he young or old?"

"Youngish, but not a teenager. Maybe around thirty?"

"Anything else?" When she shook her head, he added, "Close your eyes and replay the scene in your mind." When she closed her eyes, he said, "Now, what about his hair color? Or his height? Was he tall or short? Did he have a beard?"

She opened her eyes. "I'm not sure about any of that." Looking more troubled, she frowned. "Uncle Nate, I'm sorry. It all happened so quickly."

He reached out and gently squeezed her hand. "No, I'm sorry, honey. I didn't mean to upset you. Everything is fine."

She sighed in relief. "Oh, good."

"But, if you do happen to remember anything else, let me know, though, okay? Even if it doesn't seem important at all, it would be helpful."

"You care so much about Daniel getting pushed?"

"Yeah."

Just as she looked about to ask him why, Mitzi approached with a tray of food. Lela's French fries and malt, and his black bean burger and soup.

"Sorry about the wait. Arnold had a fresh batch of fries in the cooker. I thought you'd like them best."

"They look delicious, *danke*," Lela said.

"Of course, honey." Mitzi pointed to the bottles of mustard and ketchup at the end of the table. "Help yourself to the condiments."

"I will."

Placing his plate in front of Nate, Mitzi said, "Here you go. Not only is it loaded with veggies, I put lettuce, onion and a slice of tomato on it. Add a little bit of mustard or ketchup and you'll be in business."

"Thanks." He tried to look enthusiastic, but all he could think about was the "real" burger he was missing out on.

Looking very amused, Mitzi picked up the tray. "Just give it a try, Nate. If you hate it, I'll give you something else on the house."

"Promise?" He wouldn't make her do that no matter what, but she was easy to tease.

"For sure. I wouldn't lie to a cop."

"You knew I was a cop?"

"I might have been asking about you," she said with a bit of a saucy smile.

Unable to help himself, he watched Mitzi walk away.

Pulling his attention back to the meal, Lela giggled. "You look like you're about to eat liver and onions."

"Hey, I ordered it. I'm going to give it a try." He put a liberal dab of brown mustard on the bun, which was lightly toasted, and then took a bite.

Lela, who'd already eaten three fries, watched him. "Well?"

"It's good." He was surprised. It was way better than he'd imagined.

She giggled again. "I'm really glad you're here, Uncle Nate. I'm glad we're getting to know each other."

Happy to push all thoughts of the case to one side for a bit, he smiled at her. "I am, too. I won't stay away so long again."

"I hope not."

"I promise I won't." He just hoped that was a promise he could keep.

Chapter Twelve

Two days after Lela shared the spur-of-the-moment meal with her uncle, she was second guessing her recent choices. She wasn't used to keeping secrets from her parents. She was also sure they were not going to be pleased to find out that she'd been keeping those secrets from them.

Well, that was an understatement. They weren't going to just be displeased, they were going to be mad. That was how they were going to be.

Though a part of her wanted to shrink back into the quiet, obedient girl she used to be, Lela knew that wasn't possible. It was as if she'd crossed an imaginary threshold and come out a different person and there was no going back.

So, that made her feel strong—and rather proud of herself—but she was still worried about their reactions when they realized that she had not only spoken to Daniel several more times but also had eaten a meal with her uncle.

In addition, she was wishing she'd never said a thing

to Uncle Nate about what she thought she'd seen at the market. What if she had been completely wrong? That would be making everything in Daniel's world even muddier than it already was.

Flopping down on her back on her mattress, Lela groaned. If she made things worse for Daniel, she'd feel horrible about it.

When she heard chatter coming from the kitchen, she sat up, wondering what in the world had gotten her usually quiet mother so excited.

Faint laughter drifted down the hall, Lela knew she had to see who'd come over. Curious, she headed in that direction, craning her neck a bit to try to catch a glimpse of the visitor before she was seen.

Catching sight of a very familiar face, she grinned from ear to ear.

"Ruth! You're here!"

Her beautiful sister turned to her with a smile. "Lela, look at you. My, you've grown up."

Lela could barely believe what she was seeing. Ruth had married Jonas three years ago and moved to Berlin. She'd barely been home since. Though Lela and she often wrote, Ruth never shared too much about her life. She'd seemed rather guarded. Lela's other siblings believed it was because Ruth was simply too happy and busy being a wife and fixing up her house, but Lela had always felt like maybe there was something more going on.

She glanced at her mother. "*Mamm*, I wish you'd told me that Ruth was coming over today."

"I couldn't have told you because I didn't know she was. One moment I was washing dishes and the next she was walking through the door. You could've blown me down with a feather."

"I wanted to surprise all three of you. Where is *Daed*, by the way?"

"Your father is helping a neighbor butcher a hog today."

Ruth's expression of distaste matched Lela's own feeling. "Oh."

"You girls are always squeamish. You'll appreciate your father being there when he brings home some meat."

"To be sure." Ruth still didn't look too pleased about it, though.

Mamm scoffed. "You young girls have gotten so you don't hardly remember where your food comes from."

"I haven't forgotten where my food comes from, Mother. I just would rather go to the store and buy my meat."

"Sounds like you've gotten mighty fancy living there in Berlin."

Noticing that her sister looked crestfallen, Lela mentally sighed. Had she really imagined that things would be any different? It didn't matter how old any of them were, if they were married, or even if they didn't visit very often, their parents weren't going to change.

She decided to intervene.

"Ruth, have you been here a long time and I didn't realize it? Are you hungry?"

"I only just got here, dear. And I would love something warm to drink. It's chilly out today."

"Oh, well, then, let's give you some tea. And I made oatmeal cookies. Would you like some of those?"

"I would. *Danke*, Lela."

As Lela went to put the kettle on, *Mamm* said, "Ruth, you haven't even told me why you are here." Looking around the room, she added, "Where is your bag? How long will you be staying?"

"I'm only here because Jonas had some business with a carpenter nearby. He dropped me off here. He and the driver will be back in a couple of hours and then we'll head home."

She was so disappointed. "You aren't going to stay for a spell?"

"I'm sorry, but no."

Hurt shone in their mother's eyes. But, like always, she put on a brave front instead of revealing her sorrow. "If you are that busy, I'm surprised you had time to stop by."

Noticing that Ruth looked irritated, Lela put out three plates and napkins. "*Mamm*, would you care for a cup of tea?"

"Now? It's only two in the afternoon."

"I know. But would you?" Her mother believed in doing her chores in the middle of the day. However, she needed to make an exception. Ruth hardly ever came over. "Come sit down."

"I shouldn't. I've got quite a—"

Ruth interrupted. "Mother, please, let's have a visit." When their *mamm* still wavered, Ruth added, "Come on. Don't I matter as much as your list of chores?"

"I didn't say you didn't matter."

The kettle started to whistle. After turning off the gas stove, Lela looked back over at her mother. "*Mamm*, should I get out two cups or three?"

"Three."

Noticing how her mother didn't hesitate this time, Lela hid a smile. She wanted to spend time with Ruth, there was no doubt about that. "I'll pour three cups."

After placing a sugar bowl and a small cup of milk on the table, she placed a steaming cup of hot water and a tea bag in front of her sister.

"You've grown up," she murmured.

"Jah." Lela hoped Ruth was proud of the woman she was becoming. "I have a lot to do to be like you, though." She smiled so that Ruth would know that she meant that in the best way.

"You should only plan to be yourself," Ruth replied. "I like you already."

"Danke, Ruth."

After she served her mother and herself, Lela sat down and smiled.

"Let us bow our heads in silent prayer," *Mamm* murmured.

When their heads were lifted again, she added, "Now, tell us all about you, Ruth."

Ruth's cheeks flushed. "As you know, Jonas is busy working at the lumber mill, and I've been making the older house we bought into a home to be proud of. *Mamm*, you should see the quilt I made for our guest bedroom! It's all in shades of pink and purple and green."

"That sounds mighty bright."

"It is. It's bright and cheerful. Like a dose of sun. Jonas's mother gave us an old bedroom set. We painted the wood white. You will be very happy in the pretty room if you come to visit."

"It does sound pretty."

After adding a good dose of milk to her tea, Ruth continued, chatting all about her kitchen, the garden and the people she and Jonas had met in their church district.

Lela sipped, nibbled on cookies and was at peace with simply listening to her sister talk.

When the clock chimed three, her mother stood up. "I must get back to work on supper."

Lela stood up reluctantly. She didn't want to do anything but visit with her sister, but she also couldn't allow her mother do work by herself. "What would you like me to do, *Mamm*?

"You may go visit with Ruth. We are having a simple supper of chicken and broccoli and noodles tonight. I don't need your help."

Suddenly feeling shy, she turned to her sister. "Would you like to visit out on the front porch?"

"I would." Ruth walked over and kissed their mother's cheek. "I love you, *Mamm*."

"I love you, too, child."

As soon as they sat on the front porch, Ruth exhaled. "I've forgotten just how tense everything around here is."

Lela sat down. "Is life really that different for you in Berlin?"

"Oh, *jah*. Jonas's parents are far more easygoing. The only thing they want to know is when I'm going to give them a grandchild." Ruth chuckled. "I keep telling them that it's up to the Lord, not me."

"I wish we could see each other more often."

Ruth's expression turned more serious. "Lela, one of the reasons I wanted to visit was because I wanted you to think about coming to live with us one day."

"What? But why? I mean—"

"Hush and let me talk." Ruth lowered her voice. "If I know *Mamm*, she's going to want to be out here with us sooner than later. Or *Daed* is going to show up and then I won't get to say much at all."

"Okay..."

"Lela, dear. I know it's been hard, being the last one left at home. I just want you to know that if you would like, you are welcome to come live with Jonas and me."

"Really?"

"Really. I think it would be good for you."

"*Mamm* and *Daed* wouldn't be happy."

"I know, but you might be happier. That matters to me, Lela. What do you think?"

"I'm not sure." Honestly, she didn't even know if it was possible to be sure. Ruth's offer was a lot to think about.

Ruth's expression softened. "There would be a lot of benefits to the move, Lela. For one, you could get to know the men there. Maybe there will be someone new who catches your fancy? Or, you could get a little job at the fabric store or one of the restaurants or something."

"I don't know what to say. I mean, thank you."

"Of course, you need to stay here if that's what you want to do. I just wanted you to know that you haven't been forgotten."

"I haven't forgotten you, either." Comforted by those words, she smiled at her sister.

"So, have you met anyone you're interested in?"

Immediately she thought of Daniel. "I might have."

"Oh?" Smiling softly, Ruth leaned closer. "Well, tell me all about this man. Have I met him?"

"I don't believe so."

"Has he come over to court you?"

"*Nee.* We're keeping things quiet."

Concern entered Ruth's expression. "Why? Are you being shy? Or is he?"

"It's not that." Figuring she had nothing to lose by telling the truth, she said, "I have gotten to know Daniel Miller."

She frowned. "I don't think I know that name."

"You do. He was, uh, the talk of the town for a while. The newspapers always used all three of his names. Daniel Darrel Miller."

After another second, she gasped. "Do you mean the man who killed Brandt?"

Lela felt her stomach knot up. "He didn't kill Brandt, Ruth. He was found innocent. Someone set him up."

"But still. He shouldn't have been there…"

"Ruth, he regrets some of the decisions that he made, but that doesn't make him guilty of anything. Plus, Uncle Nate is working to find the real killer."

"How do you know?"

"I've talked to Uncle Nate."

Ruth clasped her hands together on her lap. "Is that right? How did you manage that? Did *Mamm* and *Daed* decide to accept him after all and he came over?"

"He did come over once, but it didn't go so well. You're right. *Mamm* and *Daed* have still not accepted him. But I also happened to see him when I went to BJ's Burgers on my own. I chatted with him then."

Ruth's eyes widened. "You went to the restaurant on your own? How?"

She swallowed. Her sister was turning out to be her

reality check. Lela didn't know if she was grateful for that or not. "I went after I pet sat." She held up a hand. "And before you ask more questions, yes, *Mamm* and *Daed* know that I pet sit, but *nee*, they do not know that I didn't come home right away and went to BJ's by myself."

"So, let me guess. They have no idea that you visited with Uncle Nate then, either."

"You are right. They do not."

"Oh, sister. You know better!"

"I know, but I'm tired of always following every single rule twenty-four hours a day. I need breaks."

Ruth stared at her for almost a full minute. When she spoke, her voice was low and urgent. "Lela, maybe you should come to Berlin with me and Jonas today."

"Why?"

"Because nothing is going to come of any of this. Not this relationship with Daniel Miller and not having meals with Uncle Nate. And these secrets…" She shook her head. "Lela, if *Daed* finds out you've met Uncle Nate at a restaurant he's going to punish you."

"I know he will."

"Do you, though? Because you also need to remember that he's going to be even more mad if he finds out that you've been sneaking around and seeing Daniel behind their backs." Ruth leaned forward. "*It will be bad*, Lela. Do you understand what I'm saying?"

"*Jah.*"

"If you leave today, you can start over fresh in Berlin."

Lela blinked. "Just like that?"

"Of course, just like that! All you have to do is make

up your mind. Jonas won't mind. He'll be happy to have you come home with us."

For a second she thought about it, then shook her head. What would Daniel think if she left? Or Uncle Nate? And as difficult as her parents were, she couldn't just up and leave without an explanation. "I can't, Ruth. Thank you for the offer but I need to stay here."

Something flashed in Ruth's expression. It looked a lot like regret, but she couldn't be sure. That stung. She might not see Ruth much anymore, but Lela certainly respected her. Her sister was everything she wanted to be—confident and sure of herself. And most of all, happy.

With some surprise, she realized that that's how she wanted to be. Happy. Not because she was serving other people's needs but because she was fulfilling her own.

That knowledge soothed her feelings of regret. Yes, she would have loved for Ruth to be pleased with her, but that wasn't what mattered the most.

After another second or two, her sister spoke again. "Lela, are you sure about this? Because if you're scared about talking to *Mamm*, you don't need to be. I'll—"

"I'm sure, Ruth."

Their eyes met and an understanding passed between them again. Finally, her sister nodded. "All right, then. But I sure hope you don't regret this decision, Lela. Because if *Daed* finds out and confines you to the house, you won't even be able to walk down to the phone shanty on your own. You'll be stuck here."

She'd just been thinking the same thing.

Chapter Thirteen

It was the Gingerichs' turn to host church, which made everyone happy. The yard was in perfect order, mums were artfully arranged in clay pots around the doorways, and the house was as neat as a pin.

Like always, the pews had been set up in the barn for the service, and tables and chairs had been carefully arranged in the yard for people to share a meal after the three-hour service was over.

The Gingerich family was blessed with four girls. Though their father often grumbled about always having some courting beau sitting on his front porch swing, Daniel figured on days like today the parents were grateful to have such lovely girls. They were hard workers and competent. All the food was already arranged and organized. The luncheon was going to be tasty and efficiently served. Even the most gracious attendee counted that as a blessing, because both things didn't always happen.

After saying the Lord's Prayer, Daniel sat beside Abraham as the preacher concluded the last of the service. He might have been imagining things, but the tension around him seemed to have eased a bit. He was grateful for that. He wasn't sure if it was because he'd moved out of his parents' house and they weren't actively looking like he didn't exist—or because everyone was slowly beginning to realize that he wasn't a threat to them.

The community's thawing was most likely due to men like Abraham who had wholeheartedly welcomed him back into the fold and practically dared every naysayer to change his mind.

Unable to stop himself, he looked across the space at Lela. She was sitting off to the left. She wasn't sitting with her mother. Honestly, it didn't look as if she was sitting with anyone. Instead, she'd pulled a little apart from the other women.

Though Lela was looking directly at the preacher, he could tell that her mind was someplace else. He had gotten to know her well enough to know that the slight tilt of her head and the way her expression was completely serene meant she was someplace else in her mind.

He had learned to mentally go to other places when he'd been locked up in prison. The habit had made him feel both relieved to have someplace better to fantasize about and embarrassed that he was so weak he couldn't bear to remain completely in the present.

Like everyone else, Daniel stood up again for the last prayer and closed his eyes when they were asked to give thanks. When they were dismissed, he relaxed at last. He enjoyed the sermons but it was a long time to sit on a hard wooden bench without a break.

Almost immediately, the smallest of children scampered out of the barn. The look on their parents' faces told everyone that they were glad for a moment's break, too. Though children were usually very good about sitting quietly, they were still children. He'd seen more than one mother look exhausted by the end of a long service.

Beside him, Abraham stretched his arms above his head. "It might just be me, but I'm thinking that today's sermons were better than usual. The time flew by. What do you think?"

"I liked it fine, but I couldn't say if it was better or not."

His friend laughed. "Daniel, you've become a master at keeping your thoughts and feelings to yourself."

Embarrassed by the comment, Daniel hastened to explain himself. "It's not that I'm afraid to share my thoughts, it's that I simply don't have any opinions regarding the sermons. After all, I haven't been to too many church services in years."

As they walked out of the barn and into the sunny, fall day, Abraham clasped him on the shoulder. "You've been to enough. I'm just going to say this. It's time that you stopped acting like a fugitive and began acting like you're a real part of this community."

The criticism was as unwelcome as it was surprising. "What is that supposed to mean?"

"Exactly what you think it does, Daniel. You've kept a barrier wrapped around you that's so tight, it's near impossible to let anyone in. And because of that, people aren't trusting you."

"It ain't that easy to let down my guard. You don't know how I've been treated."

Still studying him carefully, his buddy nodded. "You're right. I don't have any idea about how you were treated by the police or the lawyers or the guards or the other inmates in prison."

"Or here," he couldn't resist adding.

To his relief, Abraham didn't look offended. "*Jah.* That, too. But do I really need to have walked in your shoes in order to see that part of the problem is you? People are giving you a wide berth because you often act as if you'll get mad if they don't."

While Daniel stared at him in shock, Abraham lowered his voice. "It's time you forgive yourself, Daniel. And maybe forgive everyone else, too. You're free, you're a good man, and you have a lot to offer to the construction company, to our community and to the right woman. By acting as if you shouldn't or don't deserve to be here, you make things harder than they have to be."

He felt like rolling his eyes. "Thank you so much for feeling so free to share your opinion."

Abraham chuckled. Obviously he wasn't going to let even Daniel's sarcastic words spoil his act of kindness. Slapping Daniel on the shoulder, he grinned. "Anytime. Ah, there's Elam. I'll see you later."

He walked off before Daniel said a word, but that was probably a good thing. He wasn't sure Abraham would want to know everything he was thinking.

Honestly, he wasn't even sure that he was okay with the direction his thoughts were going. Part of him wanted to lash out and tell Abraham that he just didn't understand what it was like to be him. Yet, on the heels of that thought was the knowledge that his friend only had Daniel's best interests at heart. He'd also made a good point. Daniel had become so afraid of rejection that he kept himself closed off from everyone else.

Maybe it was time to try a little harder to assimilate again.

With that in mind, he joined the line and got a sandwich, an apple, some pasta salad and a brownie. Spying an empty seat, he walked over and sat down.

Conversation stopped among the men. One of them, Frank Gingerich, gave him a pointed look.

"Do you need me to move, Frank? Are you saving the seat for somebody?"

Frank's eyebrows lifted but he shook his head. "*Nee*. I wasna saving a spot for anyone in particular. You are welcome to sit here."

"Okay, then."

Little by little the conversation resumed. It was soon apparent that the topic of conversation was the predictions of a bad storm due to arrive later in the week. The seven men surrounding him all had opinions both on weather reports and how much preparation one needed to make for the storm.

"What do you think, Daniel?" Frank asked.

"Me? Well, ah, I guess it's all the same to me, though I'd rather do my job in dry weather than in rain or sleet."

To his surprise, a few of the men chuckled. "That's the way to think about things you cannot change. Live and learn to deal with it, ain't so?"

Daniel grinned but didn't reply immediately.

Amos, who many reckoned was approaching ninety, said, "Daniel, forgive my old brain, but I've already forgotten. Where are you working again?"

"I'm doing construction for Carter and Sons."

"An English man owns that, right?"

"That's right. A group of brothers do. They've been good to work for."

"How come you didn't choose to work for an Amish-owned company?" Amos asked.

"I chose to work for Carter and Sons because no Amish-owned company would hire me," he said, without thinking about how his statement would be received.

And, sure enough, it didn't go over well at all.

"That ain't our fault," Frank said.

Pleased he wasn't letting any of the men get him ruffled, he replied, "I didn't say it was. I was merely answering Amos's question with a truthful answer."

Frank frowned. "Still…"

Surprisingly, it was Amos who came to the rescue. "Oh, pipe down, Frank. You've got your hackles up like the man is picking a fight and that ain't the case at all. Give poor Daniel some grace, wouldja? First, when you thought the boy was guilty, you told anyone and everyone that he should go to jail. Then when he did, you seemed right smug."

Frank coughed. "I wasn't smug. I just believed that justice had been served."

"Obviously it hadn't been, since the judge and police now say Daniel Miller is innocent. Which was just like he always claimed, I might add," Amos added.

"What is your point, Amos?" Frank blurted.

"My point is that you are wanting to be your own judge and jury. You can't believe in the justice system only when it suits you, Frank." Lowering his voice, Amos said, "You canna have it both ways."

Frank looked mad enough to spit.

"I agree with Amos," a man who barely looked eighteen said. "Daniel, I'm glad you sat down with us. Time has moved on, ain't so? Besides, I have no personal grief with ya."

Other men added their agreement…and just like that the conversation moved on.

Fifteen minutes later, everyone was throwing away their trash and Daniel knew it was time to leave.

Just as he got to the end of the drive, he spied Lela again. She was standing in the shadows of a pair of blue spruces. When she saw him, she looked relieved. It was obvious that she'd been waiting for him. Taking care not to stand too close to her, he nodded politely. "Hiya, Lela."

"Hi." Looking suddenly shy, she said, "May I walk with you?"

Ah. She was ready to leave but didn't feel safe walking by herself. He'd learned enough in life to realize that it wasn't just people behind bars who enjoyed preying on anyone weaker than them. "Of course. Is there a special way you like to walk home?"

"Oh, I don't want to go home yet."

"No?"

Hope shown in her eyes. "I thought that we could perhaps go to the park for a spell. What do you think? It's not far. Plus, I doubt we'll be seeing anyone we know there."

Though he didn't have a problem not seeing her parents, it still felt a bit like a slap in the face. She was keeping him a secret. She still didn't want her family to know that she'd been talking to him.

But what could he expect? "*Jah*, sure."

It was fine, too. However, he couldn't resist wishing that their friendship had gotten to the point where they could be open about it.

Abraham had been right. He had been acting like a fugitive, always lurking in the outskirts of the community instead of making a real effort to reach out to folks. The lunch today had been a good example of that. As soon as he'd made the first step, the other men had warmed up a bit. Of course, not a lot and not every man, but it was a good start.

But perhaps, like the storm that was approaching, it was useless to fuss and stress about it. Some things simply couldn't be helped.

Letting Lela guide the way, he walked slowly next to her. Every once in a while, he had to stop and pause for a moment so she could keep up. He realized that once again, he was carrying baggage from his time in prison. He'd been surrounded by men there and had become used to walking with a purpose. Strolling along an empty road with a petite woman was very different.

The second time that happened, Lela apologized.

"I'm sorry I'm not walking faster."

"There's no reason for you to be sorry. I'm much taller than you. I've got a longer stride. Plus, we're not in a hurry. I should've been more considerate of you." He needed to remember his manners.

"I wish I was taller."

Daniel thought she was perfect the way she was. "There's nothing you can do about your height, Lela. The Lord made you the way He saw fit, *jah*?"

"I suppose so, but it doesn't stop me from wishing it, though."

"I know the feeling. Trust me, all that wishing doesn't usually make anything happen."

"I used to pray every night that the Lord would give me another two inches. When my sister Ruth overheard, she said that was a rather selfish prayer."

Daniel shrugged. "I don't know about that. I reckon a lot of prayers could be thought of as selfish. Everyone wants something. It's just some of the wants are more important than others, ain't so?"

"You're right. There are wants and needs."

"Indeed. And some people at death's door do get better. Miracles do happen." Such as the college students taking on convicted felons' cases and actually overturning everything.

She smiled up at him. "This is why I like talking with you, Daniel. You are so levelheaded."

He almost rolled his eyes, since he usually felt as if a handful of battles were constantly being waged in his head. "I don't know if anyone has ever said that about me before."

"No? What about your parents or your brother?"

"Definitely not them."

Some of the light that had been shining in Lela's eyes faded. "I'm sorry."

"Don't be. They're justified. I went through a long spurt of bad decisions. None of the things I did during that time could be classified as sensible." Hoping to encourage a smile, he added, "Now, you, on the other hand, likely make good, sensible decisions all the time."

"Me? *Nee.*" Looking pensive, she added, "Especially

not lately. I've been thinking about doing something outlandish."

"What is that?"

"Well, it's probably not very outlandish to you."

"Try me. What have you been planning?"

"My sister Ruth came over the other day and surprised me with an offer." After checking to see that she still had his attention, she added, "She suggested that I move in with her and her husband."

"Why? Are your parents in poor health?"

"*Nee.* They are strict and rather unforgiving. They seem to have gotten worse as they've grown older, too. Now there are so many rules to follow that it's a wonder I'm not always in trouble."

"What do your parents think about you moving?"

"They don't know."

They'd reached the park. It was small and empty, but rather pretty. It was obvious workers came often to plant flowers and mow and trim hedges. In the back of the space was an old metal swing set with three swings. There was also a worn-looking picnic table. "Where do you want to sit?"

"Would you mind if we sat on the swings? I'd rather move a little bit. Church was long."

"The swings work for me." After they sat on the rubber seats, he returned to their main conversation. "So, you think your parents would be against you moving?"

"I do. Very much so."

"Maybe they'd get used to it. Where does Ruth live?"

"Berlin."

"That's pretty far." He struggled to keep his expression blank. Inside, though, he was reeling. He didn't want to think about Lela being so far away. He'd never see her.

"Jah." She shrugged. "I mean, it's not that far if you are my Uncle Nate and drive a truck. But it sure is if you have only a bicycle, two feet or a horse and buggy."

"Does she need to know what you want to do soon?"

Lela darted a look at him. "Kind of."

There was something she wasn't telling him. "Why is that? What is she worried about?"

She swallowed. "You."

"Me? I don't even know her."

Looking miserable, Lela spoke again. "Ruth asked me if I was interested in anyone, and I said I might be."

"You were thinking of me?"

Blushing slightly, she nodded. "I know that was forward of me to think, and even more bold to admit such a thing face-to-face. I can't help how I feel, though."

"You honor me," he said. "Don't apologize for that."

"I don't think even my sister would be against us seeing each other. But she was right about my parents. They would be very mad."

He had known that, but hearing her state her parents' feelings so openly was disappointing.

Maybe if Abraham hadn't given him the pep talk just an hour ago he would've accepted Lela's choice to continue hiding their friendship. But the lunch with the men had changed things. Or, maybe he liked Lela so much that he was willing to fight for her. He wanted to be able to court her at her house. He wanted to be able to talk to her after a church service.

He really didn't want to only get to spend time with

her in deserted parks. He'd been through too much to be okay with that.

Deciding to be completely honest, since he had nothing to lose, he got off the swing and stood in front of her.

"Lela, I'm going to be honest with you. I hope that's all right."

Her pretty brown eyes widened. "Of course it is."

He took a deep breath, said a quick prayer for strength and then spoke. "I like you."

Smiling, she stood up. After two steps, they were standing just inches apart. So close that he could smell the floral scent of her shampoo. Close enough to notice that she had a very faint spray of freckles on her nose.

Close enough to notice that her lips were parted, they looked soft, and she wouldn't be upset if he leaned down and kissed her softly.

It would be so easy to kiss her.

"Daniel, I like you, too. But that's been obvious, right?"

"It is. And I'm honored by your regard. But... I don't want to sneak around to see you."

"But I don't have a choice."

She looked crushed, but he couldn't back down. He had to stand up for himself, even when his heart was involved.

Maybe especially when his heart was involved.

"*Nee*, I think you do."

"What are you saying?"

"I'm saying that I've been through too much to continue to sneak around like a criminal, Lela. A friend reminded me today that I can't be accepted into the fold if I keep holding myself apart from it. And that's what I would be doing if we didn't come clean with your parents."

"They'll be mad. They'll make me stay in the house for weeks."

"I'll come with you and talk to them, too."

She shook her head. "My parents won't listen to a word you say. I'm sorry, but you don't understand what you're asking me to do."

"I'm sorry, but I feel the same way." When she gaped at him, he added, "I've already been locked up. People have already ignored me when I spoke the truth. Fighting for myself…and fighting to survive behind bars was difficult. If I can do that, then I think you can be honest with your parents."

Tears filled her eyes. "Daniel."

"Lela, do you really think that no one is going to ever see us together? Do you actually imagine that waiting for me behind shadows after church can go on for very long?"

"I… I don't know." A teardrop slid down her cheek and broke his heart. But he couldn't back down. He wanted to be with her, but he wanted to be with her for real. As her boyfriend. As her fiancé. As her husband.

Even if the Lord decided that they were destined to break up and marry other people, Daniel knew that the way they were going couldn't continue. No matter what, he didn't want to be someone's dirty secret. He didn't know a lot, but he knew that he deserved more than that.

She hiccupped. "Daniel, I don't know what to do."

"Let's take it one step at a time, then." He reached for her hand. It was chilly and he hated that. "Would

you like me to come over this evening and tell them
the news with you?"

"You want to have this conversation tonight?"

"Of course tonight." He rubbed her palm, trying to
warm it a bit. "I'm not going to let you fret and worry
for days. You'll get an ulcer or some such."

A hint of a smile returned. "I don't think I'm in danger of ulcers."

He certainly hoped not, but he cared so much about
her, he didn't even want her to lose a minute of sleep
worrying. "What do you say?"

"I guess I don't have a choice, do I?"

"Of course you do. You can do anything you want.
We can wait as long as you want until you feel comfortable."

"I want to feel comfortable now."

She was so earnest, he decided to push her just a
little bit. Taking a deep breath, he plunged in. "Lela,
you are in charge. Your happiness matters to me. It
matters a lot."

"Your opinion matters to me, too."

"Okay. If you're being honest, then I have to tell ya
that I don't want to sneak around or hide. We'll tell your
parents we want to be together, and I'll stay by your side
so you don't have to be afraid."

She sighed. "All right. Let's do this tomorrow night,
then."

He couldn't believe it. "All right? Really?"

Smiling, she nodded. "Really. But if I'm locked in my
room for days and weeks, it's going to be all your fault."

"If you're locked in your room, I'll find a way to rescue you and take you to your sister's house."

She swiped her cheek with her free hand. "You'd really do that, wouldn't you?"

"Of course." Leaning down, he kissed her on the cheek. "I really like you, Lela. Now, let's get you headed home. I'll come over at six tonight."

"I'll be ready."

Her voice was strained. She sounded like she was going into battle. But maybe she was. *"Gut,"* he said simply. There was really nothing else to say.

They left the park and walked together until they reached a cross street. "Keep your faith, Lela. We can do this."

"I sure hope so. I'm going to start praying now."

"I will, too." After they parted, Daniel decided to make one more stop before he went to his garage apartment at Abraham's. He was going to pay a call on the bishop. If the man was available, Daniel was going to ask him to join the conversation. At the very least, it would help make sure Lela's parents wouldn't kick him out of the house the moment he arrived.

Chapter Fourteen

The waiting was horrible. No, wondering if Daniel was actually coming over was horrible. Lela wouldn't have been surprised if he'd changed his mind, but she knew she'd be disappointed if he had. It felt as if she'd been waiting for someone to believe in for her entire life. Now the Lord had given her Daniel.

At least, she'd hoped that was the case.

But still, time passed too slowly.

All day long, she'd stayed near the house and helped her mother cook and mop the wood floors. Then she'd decided that, if Daniel was actually going to come over, the living room tables needed to be polished and the area rug shaken out.

When she still had too much time on her hands, she made pumpkin bars. Maybe Daniel would get to stay long enough to eat a treat before her parents threw him out.

It was a blessing that her father had been out in the fields most of the day and her mother was in the base-ment organizing some fabric and all the canning supplies. Otherwise, she would have asked Lela far too many questions that she would be reluctant to answer.

All too soon, it was time to start preparing supper, which was a simple meal of scrambled eggs with vegetables, bacon and fresh biscuits.

As the three of them ate the meal in near silence, Lela watched the clock. When it turned a quarter after five, she knew she'd get sick if she ate another bite.

Her father noticed. "What's wrong, Lela? Why aren't you eating?"

"Nothing's wrong. I'm simply not too hungry."

"Why not?"

"I don't know."

"It's not right for you to waste the food. Eat some more."

She moved the food around her plate and only took the smallest bite.

Her mother glanced at her curiously before picking up the cloth-covered basket of biscuits. "Would you like another biscuit, Elam?"

"*Nee*, Charity."

She lifted the platter of bacon. "A piece of bacon, perhaps?"

"*Nee*. I have had enough." He pushed back his chair and walked outside.

Lela sighed in relief. No doubt her father was going to go to the barn and check on the animals.

Unbelievably, another fifteen minutes had passed. Her stomach churned. Why in the world had she given in to Daniel? She did want everything out in the open, but the waiting was awful.

Feeling the weight of her mother's steady gaze, Lela

stood up and grabbed her plate. "I think I'll get started on the dishes."

"Just a moment, Lela."

She turned back to the table. "Yes? May I get you something?"

One eyebrow rose. "Beyond what is on this table? *Nee*. I'd much rather you tell me what has gotten you in such a state."

"Ah, I'm not sure what you mean." She glanced at the clock again.

"Lela, why are you continually looking at the clock this evening? Why did you make pumpkin bars? Why did you polish all the furniture in the living room?"

And…now she felt like sinking to the floor. "I didn't think you noticed."

"I noticed." *Mamm* folded her arms across her chest. "Lela, stop procrastinating and just tell me what is going on."

"Fine. A man is coming over tonight." Unable to help herself, she glanced at the clock again. "At six."

"You have a caller?" Her mother turned to look up at the clock. "And he's coming in twenty minutes?"

"Jah."

Twin spots of color bloomed on her cheeks. "Oh, my word." She got to her feet. "Why didn't you tell me? We could've eaten earlier!" Picking up her dish and the platter of eggs, her mother hurried into the kitchen. "Go get the other dishes. I'll start washing."

Lela did as her mother bid, but she felt as if there was a ticking time bomb in the house. Just waiting for the right moment to explode.

Buoyed by years of experience doing the dishes

together, she and her mother worked in unison. Lela brought in dishes, cleared the plates and handed each to her mother. *Mamm*, in turn, washed each piece and set it on the rack on the counter to dry. The effort took only ten minutes.

Now there was only ten minutes to go.

Lela needed a break. "I'm going to go to my room."

"Hold on, now. Should I put on *kaffi*?"

"I don't know."

Mamm nibbled her bottom lip. "It's been a few years since one of your sisters had a beau over. I seem to be a little rusty." After a pause, she said, "You know what? I think I am going to make a fresh pot of coffee. It's chilly out, ain't so?"

Before Lela could fit in a word, she continued. "Even if your beau doesn't want anything warm to drink, your father will like that." She smiled. "He's going to need some sustenance when he realizes that his youngest might soon be leaving the nest."

Leaving the nest? This was getting worse and worse. "I really need to go down the hall."

"Hold on." Rinsing out the percolator, she said, "I just realized that you never said who your caller was. Who is it?"

"Daniel Miller."

"Daniel? Hmm. Who... Wait a moment. Daniel Darrel Miller? Your cousin's murderer?" She turned to stare at Lela.

"He didn't murder anyone, *Mamm*."

The filter that she'd been cleaning fell into the sink as her mother pressed both hands to her much paler face. "Lela, what have you done?"

What could she say? That she was halfway to falling in love with the man? Her mouth went dry. "I…"

A knock sounded at the door.

Lela's heart felt like it was beating so fast Daniel
could probably hear it from outside the house. "I better go get it."

"Nee."

"Mamm, Daniel is here. I'm letting him in."

Her mother hurried to her side and grabbed her arm.
"Wait. What is your father going to say?"

"I guess we're about to find out."

"But—"

"It's too late to stop me, *Mamm*. I invited Daniel, he
came over, and I'm going to open the door."

She pushed past her mother just as another knock
came.

Mentally praying for help, she opened the door.

And…there was Daniel. He was dressed in clean
gray pants, a long-sleeved dark blue shirt and thick
black leather boots. His cheeks were freshly shaved and
his eyes were fastened on her. "Good evening, Lela."

"Good evening, Daniel." When she heard a subtle
clearing of a throat, she realized that she'd completely
ignored Bishop Schlabach! "Bishop! I'm so sorry!
Please come in."

"Not a problem, Lela," the kind man murmured as
he led the way inside. "You can call me Joe, though,
jah? I'm only here as a friend tonight."

She honestly didn't know if she could ever call him
Joe, but she nodded. *"Wilcom* to our home. Please come
into the living room." She looked around, expecting her

mother to be standing in the middle of the entryway, but she was nowhere to be found.

"Danke." Taking off his hat and shrugging off his coat, he wandered over to the couch.

Daniel paused. "Are you okay?"

Lela shrugged. "I'm not sure, but bringing the bishop here is genius."

He smiled slightly. "I thought maybe your parents might let me stay long enough to plead my case if I brought support."

"Let's hope so." Following the men into the living room, she said, "I made pumpkin bars, and I believe *mei mamm* made *kaffi*. Would either of you like a cup?"

"That sounds mighty nice, Lela. I'll have a cup," Bishop Schlabach said.

"For me, as well," Daniel said.

"I'll be right back." She hurried to the kitchen, praised the Lord that her mother had put the percolator on the stove and got out three coffee cups. She usually didn't drink coffee at night, but she figured she was likely going to be up all night, anyway. After filling the cups and setting them on a tray, she added some napkins and the plate of pumpkin bars.

The kitchen door swung open and in walked both of her parents.

"Lela, what is going on?" her father asked in a dark tone. "Did you truly invite Daniel Miller into my home?"

For a second, she wavered, then figured there was no denying the truth.

Therefore, she turned to face them, lifted her chin

and said the only thing she possibly could. "Yes, I did. He's sitting in the living room with Bishop Schlabach. Would you care to join us?"

Chapter Fifteen

Sometimes, when Daniel was having trouble going to sleep, he would lie in bed and think about a future with Lela. It would be a good one. He could see himself coming home from a construction job—maybe even after spending a long day on the roof of some house. He'd arrive home tired and sore. Then, when he walked in the door, he'd see her in the kitchen.

Even though he'd never seen her actual living space, he could imagine what she would like. There'd probably be a candle burning. Maybe she'd be humming a tune while tending to two pans on the stove. Or, perhaps, Lela would be fretting about the bread rising or the water boiling. Of course, there would be a dog of indiscriminate breed lying in the middle of the floor. It would likely be in the way, but she wouldn't care. Instead, she'd simply step over the thing as she worked and fussed.

She would be adorable.

Of course, no late night fantasy would be complete without him walking in to meet her. Because then—in his dream at least—Lela would hear his footsteps, put whatever was in her hands on the counter and turn to greet him.

And when she did, Lela would smile brightly. Like he was worth something.

Daniel knew that if he had such a thing to look forward to every evening, then he would be a blessed man, indeed. He would live for her smiles and for her happiness. Simply being around her would make his heart lift.

And what would he do in return for her giving him so much? Why, he would take care of her. He'd work hard and make sure she had everything she needed. He'd look after her—just the way she looked after him. And when they went out in the world, he'd keep close by, because he now had firsthand knowledge of the things that men could do...if they had a mind to do bad things.

Yes, he'd always imagined he'd be the strong one in the marriage. The protector. The provider. She would need him. His mind would form such a perfect picture of matrimonial bliss, it would encourage the memories from prison to fade away.

But now, sitting down in her parents' living room, watching her practically dare her father to raise a fuss or say something cruel, Daniel realized that he'd had it all wrong. He might have bigger muscles, but Lela was absolutely the stronger one. She might have hidden it well under her smiles and fondness for dogs, but inside where it mattered, Lela possessed a spine of steel.

He couldn't be prouder of her.

And, maybe, feel a little unworthy of her love.

For what felt like a full minute after Lela had announced that the bishop had come over with him, the silence stretched so tight one could have bounced a penny on it.

"Elam, either help your daughter with the tray or get out of her way, *jah*?" Joe asked. "The poor thing is holding three cups of coffee and a plate of cookies. It's bound to be heavy."

Daniel leaped to his feet. "I'll take it, Lela."

Elam stepped forward, his expression like ice. "*Nee*. I will help."

Instead of accepting either of their assistance, she walked the last four steps to the coffee table and set it down herself. "*Danke*, bishop, but I'm stronger than I look."

Unable to help himself, Daniel smiled to himself as he sat back down. He'd just been thinking that very thing.

"Have a seat, child, and take your *kaffi*, too. Daniel and I can pick up our cups ourselves."

Elam was still standing. "Where is my coffee, daughter?"

"I have ours," Charity said as she approached. "Please sit down, Elam." When he sat, she handed him his mug and then took the last empty chair.

After another fortifying sip of the hot beverage, Daniel knew he could no longer delay the purpose of the visit. "Elam and Charity, I would like to court your daughter."

"*Nee,*" Elam said.

Daniel felt his cheeks heat with a combination of irritation and embarrassment. After quickly glancing at Lela, he reminded himself that he'd been through many things far worse than this.

With that in mind, he sat up straighter and pled his case. "I realize that I might need to prove myself to you both, but I'm willing to do that. Lela is worth doing whatever it takes to overcome your objections."

Charity looked at her husband.

Elam put his cup down. "There is no reason for you to do whatever you think will make a difference. You will never be welcome in this house, and you will certainly never be good enough for our daughter."

The bishop, who'd just eaten half of one of the pumpkin bars, put the rest of it down with a sigh. "Hold on, Elam," he said. "You are being unfair. There is no doubt that Daniel is not responsible for Brandt's death. He was unjustly imprisoned."

"The courts could've been wrong."

"They were not. The evidence is solid. I spoke to the detective on the case."

"You spoke to Nate?" Charity asked.

"I did. He explained all the evidence to me in some detail. I'm sure he'd be glad to explain it to you, too."

"He is not welcome in this home, Bishop," Elam said.

Looking visibly irritated, Bishop Schlabach crossed his legs. "You are unwilling for your *frau* to see her own brother? For your daughter to know her uncle?"

"I have my reasons."

"*Nee.* You are being foolishly obstinate."

Charity inhaled sharply as the tension in the room heightened even further.

"Joe, I respect you, but you are not right." He lifted his chin. "Besides, this is my house."

"This is your house, but there are two young people sitting here with us who should have a say in the matter," Joe countered. "Lela, what do you think, child? Would you like Daniel to court ya?"

"She doesn't need to answer," Charity blurted.

"*Mamm*, I am right here. I can speak for myself." Setting down the mug she'd been holding between her hands, she said, "*Jah*, Bishop. I would like Daniel to court me. I think he's very nice."

"How would you even know what he's like?" her father scoffed. "You haven't even had the opportunity to speak to him." When Daniel realized she was about to reveal just how many times they'd talked, he blurted, "That is why I'd like the opportunity to formally court Lela. We could get to know each other here, with your supervision."

Joe smiled. "That seems reasonable, ain't so?"

"*Nee*," Lela said. "Because, you see… Daniel and I already have had several occasions to talk. I've spent time with him after church on two different occasions."

Her mother blinked. "How could that be?" Before Lela could answer, she glared at Daniel. "What have you been doing? Lurking around, just waiting to make your move?"

This was going so badly. Shaken that Lela seemed intent on sharing everything, he shook his head. "I have not been lurking anywhere. She and I happened to see each other when we were both walking."

"Happened, my foot," Elam muttered.

"You're right, *Daed*," Lela said. "There was no happenstance about it. I pursued him."

The whole room froze. Even the bishop appeared taken aback. As for himself, he was torn between want-

ing to motion for Lela to stop talking and pride that she
was putting everything out in the open.

"She did approach me first, but I didn't try very hard
to dissuade her," he murmured. "Lela has a way about
her that I canna look away from. It's like she's the sun
and I've been in the dark for far too long."

When Elam appeared about to speak again, Joe interrupted. "Lela, I wish you hadn't gone against your
parents' wishes, but I do understand."

"*Danke*, Bishop."

"I surely don't," her father said. "And Daniel, I don't
care if you think she's the sun and moon combined, you
may not court her."

Lela stood up. "Then I guess I'll have to leave."

Her mother gaped. "Where are you going?"

"Ruth asked me to move in with her and Jonas. I told
her I'd need time to think about it. After today, I don't
need any more time."

Her father turned to her *mamm*. "Did you know about
this?"

"You know I did not."

"I'm going to see Daniel with or without your permission, *Daed*," Lela said as she put her hands on her
hips. "I care about him, and you aren't basing your decision on anything other than your own personal prej-
udice."

"He is a killer."

"Uncle Nate says he isn't."

"That's what you've heard. You don't really know
what Nate thinks."

"Actually, I do. I sat with him at a restaurant the other
day and spoke to him," Lela fired back.

When her mother started crying, the bishop seemed uncomfortable, too.

As for Lela, she looked far too alone.

Getting to his feet, he disregarded everything her parents had said and walked toward her and put out his arms. Without a second's hesitation, she walked into his arms and clung.

"I'm sorry," she whispered. "There were too many secrets. I couldn't hold all of that inside anymore."

"I understand. It's all right."

The bishop got to his feet and stood in front of her parents. "If you're looking for evidence, it's right in front of you. These two are already a couple. It's obvious that your daughter has a choice, and she will choose Daniel. In addition, even Ruth knows you are being too harsh. She's going to give Lela shelter."

Elam shook his head.

Looking disappointed, Joe turned to Lela. "Child, go get your things. Daniel and I will help you carry them to the buggy. When we get to my house I'll help you get a driver to take you to Ruth's."

"All right." Looking up at Daniel, she said, "I'll be right back."

Charity stood up. "Wait!"

Lela turned on her heel. *"Mamm?"*

"You don't have to go, dear. You may see Daniel." She swallowed. "As long as everything is proper, I have no worries."

"This is not your decision, Charity," Elam said.

In a firm tone, she replied, "I'm not losing a daughter for your pride. I won't. Bishop is right. We can either accept Daniel and his request to court Lela properly, or we will lose her. I'm not going to lose her."

One second passed. Then two. At last, he spoke. "She may stay."

"Because?" Bishop Schlabach pressed.

"Because Daniel may court her."

"Danke," Daniel murmured.

Of course, at the moment, he wasn't sure who he was thanking. Was it Elam? Charity, Joe or Lela? Or was it the almighty God, who had to have been watching out for him and Lela?

Definitely the Lord.

No, actually, it was all of them. Of late, he'd come to realize that he had much to be thankful for. Maybe more than he'd ever realized.

Chapter Sixteen

From the moment he'd taken on Brandt's cold case, Nate felt as if he'd become consumed by it. Though he'd started with that first interview with Elam, Charity and Lela, he'd talked to countless other people. Some folks had been eager to help. Others had made sure he'd been aware of their distaste of the efforts that had been done. Others had simply refused to speak to him.

It hadn't only been the Amish who had been close-mouthed, either. Suspicion of the police crossed practically every age, religious belief or ethnicity line.

It was nothing that he hadn't come across before.

However, this time he viewed everyone's opinions with a new perspective—because he, too, had lost someone in his family. He had also been dismayed by Peck's lack of thorough investigation.

However, as he sat in a corner booth with Mitzi, Nate was coming to realize that there had also been hidden blessings to this case: he'd met someone whom he really cared about. Mitzi was everything he'd dreamed of finding. She was kind and knew how to tell a good joke. She listened attentively and was open about herself. She also had a deep faith that wasn't instantly apparent but always seemed to lie just below the surface. He appreciated that.

Of course, he would also be lying if he'd said that he'd never noticed her outward appearance. Mitzi was slim, tall and athletic. She didn't wear a lot of makeup and kept her hair short because she didn't want to fuss with it much. Though she'd once joked about her figure, saying that she had fewer curves than a teenaged boy, he thought she was perfect.

When he'd told her that, she'd laughed him off.

She wasn't laughing at the moment, however. Instead, she was looking at him with concern as she sipped her coffee.

Feeling self-conscious, he wiped his mouth. Maybe he'd had a crumb or something he hadn't realized?

Her expression didn't change.

"What's wrong?" he finally asked.

"How about you tell me? You don't seem like your usual self this afternoon." Her blue eyes filled with compassion. "Is everything okay, Nate?"

"With us? It's perfect, though I was just thinking that it's time I took you on a proper date."

She smiled. "I'd like that."

"Yeah? Fantastic. Where do you want to go?"

"I'm easy to please. How about anywhere but here?"

He chuckled. "Deal. I'll text you tonight with some suggestions and nights I'm available this week. Hopefully one evening will work for you."

"I'll make one of them work, even if I have to call some other servers and beg."

"I'm thrilled about that, Mitzi. I really enjoy being with you, and I can't wait to take you out on a real date."

"I'm looking forward to that, too." As their eyes met, her smile slipped a little. "Nate, as happy as I am to be making plans with you, I'm not thrilled that I still don't know what's put the shadows under your eyes. What's going on?"

"It's this case I'm on." Seeing that her expression didn't change, he added, "I'm feeling at a loss of what to do. I've interviewed dozens of people, talked to Daniel and looked at every piece of evidence that was found at the scene. Unfortunately, the man I'm looking for seems to have been vanished into thin air."

"Really? Are you sure you aren't just looking for the wrong person?"

"I could be," he allowed, "but I doubt it. You see, Daniel is very sure about this suspect's appearance. It's unusual enough that he should stick out, especially in an Amish community. Most of the folks I've talked to don't even seem to recognize his description. The only people who did know who I was talking about were the few kids I could find who had been at the party."

"And…?"

"And they haven't seen him since that night. It's like he vanished into thin air."

Mitzi waved her hand. "Maybe it's not that complicated. It could just be that he's gone. Maybe your suspect got scared and ran. Why, he could be living someplace across the country. That happens, right?"

Nate nodded slowly. "That doesn't fit in this case, though. Daniel and Lela believe they saw him at the farmers market."

"Oh, wow. Do you think they were telling you the truth?"

"Yes. Lela told me that this guy pushed Daniel down to the ground. She had no reason to lie."

Mitzi leaned back in her seat and crossed her arms over her chest. "That's a tough one, isn't it? It's like he donned a disguise and then darted in the woods or something and became something else."

Donned a disguise. "There are a lot of places around here that he could do that, aren't there?" he said slowly.

"I think so. I reckon any vacant area or corner could do the trick." When he continued to stare at her, she unfolded her arms. "Sorry. I guess you can tell that I've been watching way too many detective shows on my nights off."

The thought of her sitting on her couch trying to solve mysteries made him smile. "I didn't know you liked cop shows."

"Nate, come on. You're a cop!" She winked. "You didn't think I only liked you for your good looks and charm, did you?"

"Kind of." He laughed. "So, you're saying that if I was a farmer I would've been out of luck?"

"I can't lie, you might have been," she teased. "Of course now I'm starting to think I should've checked your badge. You know, you can't trust everyone about what they say their story is."

Playing along, he pulled out his wallet and showed her his badge. "Here you go. Study it all you want."

To his surprise, she picked it up and studied it closely. "Hmm. For some reason, I had been sure your real name was Nathan."

"Nope. It's Nate."

"And you don't have a middle name, so you can't be going by that. I also thought that maybe your first name was Jonathan or something."

"You sound almost disappointed that I'm just 'Nate.'"

"I'm not disappointed at all. It's just… Well, I guess my mind sometimes jumps around and thinks about how some people aren't exactly who they seem to be at first glance."

Nate wasn't sure if he was impressed or a little worried that she had such a suspicious mind. "You have been watching a bunch of cop shows."

"I can't help it. I see all kinds of folks in here and talk to almost everyone. Not everyone likes to put their whole self out there. Just part of it."

"Hey, Mitzi?" BJ called out from the beverage station. "Sorry, but I need you back."

"All right!" She pressed her hands on the surface of the table. "I guess it's time. I'm sorry."

He pressed one hand over hers. "There's nothing to apologize about. I'm glad you could fit me in. I'll call you later."

She turned her palm over so their fingers could link for an instant before she pulled her hand away. "I'll look forward to it. Be safe, cop."

"Always. You, too."

Mitzi winked before turning away.

Nate sipped his glass of water as he watched her speak to BJ, put her apron back on, then greet a couple standing at the front of the restaurant.

Now that he knew her better, he realized that his first impression was that she was a pretty server with a great smile. He still thought both of those things, but now he was aware of her many other qualities, too—one of which was that she didn't trust easy.

Suddenly, he realized that Mitzi might have just given him the spark he'd needed to locate this mysterious Wyatt Troyer.

Maybe he'd been looking at this guy all wrong. He'd assumed that he was Amish because Daniel had been adamant that he was.

But what if Wyatt had fooled Daniel?

What if Wyatt wasn't Amish at all? What if he was as English as Mitzi and had adopted an Amish disguise in order to gain the trust of naive Amish teenagers like Daniel had been?

Thinking about it harder, Nate decided that made a lot of sense. Wyatt could be from a community with a lot of Amish and had learned some Pennsylvania Dutch phrases. He could have bought some Amish clothes, too. And, if he was pretending to be in the middle of his *rumspringa*, no Amish teenagers would question his ability to drive a car. Why, the other teens probably wouldn't have second-guessed a lot of things Wyatt was doing, because they were doing crazy things, too.

It would be the perfect cover.

Now all he had to do was figure out who he really was.

Nate rolled his eyes. Yeah, that was all he had to do.

Figuring out that should only take another couple of months, if he was lucky.

Chapter Seventeen

Four days had passed since Daniel and Bishop Schlabach came over and spoke to Lela's parents. To Lela's mind, however, it might as well have been a whole year.

After the guests had left, it was obvious that neither of her parents were quite sure about what to do with her. On one hand, they were both very cross with her. However, on the other hand, they realized that she'd grown up and had a mind of her own. After several conversations, her father finally gave Daniel permission to pay a call. It went so well that her mother asked Daniel to come over again soon.

And now, here they were, out on the streets near her home in a courting buggy! Lela was thrilled about that.

She was not as thrilled about being Daniel's passenger, however.

It was very obvious that Daniel had little experience in driving one. Sable, the trusty Tennessee walking horse who took just about everything in stride, was looking extremely put upon. Lela feared that she was either going to stop walking altogether, or head home, with or without Daniel's directions on the reins.

As they moved to a stop again, Daniel pulled on the reins and set the brake. "I'm sorry, Lela. It seems I'm a miserable buggy driver."

"At least you admit it," she teased.

He cast her a sideways glance. "That's all you can say?"

"Not at all. It is, however, all I dare say out loud."

He lifted an eyebrow. "Because?"

"Because if I say what I'm actually thinking, I will likely hurt your feelings."

He frowned. "You have that much criticism?"

Realizing that his feelings really were a little bruised, she tried to temper herself. "Daniel, I'm sorry, but I'm afraid so. You're not a very good buggy driver. It's a fact."

"*Jah.* I guess it is." After making sure that they were still alone on the road, he rubbed his chin. "I can't believe I am struggling so much with this buggy, but I guess it couldn't be helped. Before *rumspringa* I was too young to drive a buggy. Then, during my run-around years, I didn't want to learn much about courting buggies. I did whatever I could to stay off the farm. And then…" His voice drifted off.

There was no need for him to finish. They both knew what had happened after that.

"It's all right. It just takes time and practice."

"I reckon so."

When Sable shook her head a bit and scraped at the ground with a hoof, Daniel frowned. "I could be wrong, but I think Sable isn't real pleased with this outing."

"Sorry, but I know she isn't. She's a very good horse and usually mild mannered. But I fear she isn't enjoying your heavy hand on the reins."

"Really? You already know what I'm doing wrong?"

"I'm afraid it's rather obvious." Honestly, she was fairly sure even the smallest Amish child would know that Daniel needed to be lighter in his directions.

"Would you like to drive the buggy back to your house?"

"Are you serious?"

"Of course. You seem to know what the horse needs and likes. You're the better driver."

Lela knew she was. But she said, "You aren't afraid of someone seeing me driving you around?"

His expression turned soft as he reached for her hand. "Why would I be afraid? Because I'm the man and you're the woman?"

"Well, *jah*." Most men would never allow their pride to take such a hit.

"First, I don't care if the whole world sees you driving me around in a courting buggy. *Nee*, that's not true. I'd *love* for everyone to see that. Because then that would mean that everyone would know that I was the man you chose to spend time with. I'm very proud about that."

"Come on. You know what I mean."

"I don't need to make myself feel better by driving you, Lela. Back in prison, I had some scary and not-fun moments, but I also learned quite a few things. I learned to read the Bible more—and to not only read it but *think* about the words I was reading. Do you know what I mean?"

She nodded.

"I also received some counseling sessions from a very wise man who reminded me not to look for gratification and acceptance in the wrong places. I'm not going to worry about what some people who don't like me in the first place are going to think about me being a passenger."

"Well, that is a healthy way to look at things."

"I think so, too. It certainly helps me to not worry about things I cannot change. I can't suddenly become a good buggy driver, Lela. I'm certainly not going to risk either your safety or Sable's mouth by being too stubborn."

"All right, then."

"Let's switch spots. The brake is on."

Of course, he hopped right out. It took her a moment to situate the skirts of her dress so she wouldn't trip over the hem while she climbed out.

But it turned out that she didn't have to worry about tripping after all. Daniel was right there, and before she knew it, he had his hands on her hips and was practically lifting her out of her seat.

No, he was. She wasn't exactly a tiny woman, but he was lifting her as if she weighed nothing at all! She rested her hands on his shoulders as he transported her to the ground. "Daniel, you didn't have to pick me up."

"I know." He grinned. "But how could I pass up the opportunity? It's not too often a man gets an opportunity to hold his sweetheart for a moment."

He thought of her as his sweetheart? Staring at him, she whispered, "What are you saying?"

Some of the humor faded from his expression. "I think you know, Lela."

"I am guessing. I need you to tell me, though."

"All right." He swallowed. "What I'm saying is that I already think of you as mine. Um, that doesn't mean that you have to feel the same way, though."

A shiver ran through her. A shiver that didn't have anything to do with nervousness and had everything to do with happiness. Of course she felt the same way. But did she really want to open her heart to him and reveal it?

Looking into his eyes, she realized that she had no choice. He needed her as much as she needed him. And he needed her words, too.

"I do feel the same way."

A small smile appeared, then gradually slid into a bright grin. "Yeah?"

"Of course, yes. Daniel, you already know how much I like you. I think I like being your sweetheart, too."

"I hoped you did." He shook his head. "But sometimes every doubt and insecurity that I feel seems to show up in spades. I start wondering why a woman like you would ever want to settle for a man like me."

If it was the last thing she did, she was going to help him see his worth. "*A man like you?* Daniel, you are so strong. And not just because you can carry me around, either. You're strong on the inside, too. You survived so many bad things and yet you aren't harsh and bitter. You haven't used your past as a reason to not try to change the future. I think you're wonderful."

He stared at her. For once, his firm control on his

emotions was relaxed and a myriad of emotions filled his eyes. Longing, care, temptation. Fear.

She recognized each one because she was feeling the exact same way. From practically the first moment they'd started to talk, she'd been drawn to him. Yes, she'd felt sorry for everything that he'd been through and wanted to comfort him and be his friend.

But she couldn't deny that there was more between them than just a willingness to lend a helping hand. He'd sparked something deep inside her that she hadn't known existed. Until she met him, she hadn't even realized that she would ever want such things.

Unable to look away, she gazed into his eyes. Her breath hitched. Startled, she realized that her lips were parted. Hastily, she closed her mouth again.

What in the world was wrong with her?

Some of the doubtful expression that Daniel had worn faded. He smiled.

"What?" she asked.

He reached for her right hand. Gave a little tug, then pulled her closer. Now their bodies were practically touching. She had to lift her chin to meet his gaze.

"I… I thought maybe I was the only one," he murmured. "I thought that maybe I was thinking things that would scare you. Or get my cheek slapped."

She was confused. "I haven't slapped anyone in my life."

An eyebrow rose. "No? Well, then that's a good sign for me, I reckon." Lowering his voice, he released her hand in order to bring both of his to her face.

One of his thumbs swiped her cheek. "Your skin is so soft."

She trembled from his gentle touch.

He noticed. Something new flickered in his gaze. "Maybe I should change my mind. Or maybe I should ask, but I just can't. I'm sorry, Lela, I just can't wait another moment."

Still cradling her face in between his hands, he leaned down and kissed her.

She wasn't stunned or shocked or scared. It might have taken her a moment to figure out what he had in mind, but once she did, there was no way she was going to shy away.

The truth was that she wanted this kiss. She wanted her first kiss to come from him. His touch was light. Soft and gentle. Barely a press.

Lifting his head, he said, "Okay?"

Was she supposed to speak now? *"Jah."*

He smiled again before kissing her again. When one of his hands pressed between her shoulder blades, she reached out and held his arms.

Hoped he'd never let her go.

She might be naive and innocent, but she was no fool. Kissing Daniel Darrel Miller had been a wonderful thing. Special and perfect.

Already, she hoped it would happen again.

Chapter Eighteen

Daniel had no idea where he'd found the strength to move away from Lela and act as if his life hadn't just changed.

All right, so that might have been a bit too dramatic way of describing things, but the sentiment was there nonetheless. For so long—even before he'd met Wyatt and ruined his life—he'd felt uncertain about himself. He'd always felt a bit "less than" and awkward, even when he knew he wasn't any worse or different than most other boys his age. He supposed one of the counselors he'd spoken with in prison would say that his low self-esteem had led to his need to befriend Wyatt and do things that he knew were unhealthy and harmful.

Maybe that was right. He didn't know.

All he did know was that from the time he first saw Lela at the farmers market, he'd known she was out of his league. She was sheltered and sweet. He was not.

But more than that, she saw the good in people. In everyone, including him.

Now that she'd shared that she cared about him,

cared enough to let him kiss her? Well, he knew that he wasn't going to be able to ever go back. She was his girl now. One day, if the Lord was good and if her parents would consent, then she would be his wife.

"Are you still fine with me driving you, Daniel?"

"Of course. You do a good job with the horse." With a smile, he added, "Sable seems much happier."

"The trick, I think, is to have a light touch." With her left hand, she pointed to the way her right was holding the reins before returning to hold both pieces of leather with both hands. "Sable knows that I'm comfortable, so she is comfortable, too."

"She can get that just from the way you hold the reins?"

"Absolutely."

He thought her earnest confidence was adorable. "Who taught you how to drive a buggy? Your mother or your father?"

"Neither. My sisters. Because I'm the youngest, my parents always seemed perfectly happy to let either my brothers or my sisters look after me."

"They didn't mind?"

She shook her head. "I was like their doll at first." She chuckled. "And then, later on, they did their best to help me so I wouldn't have to be stuck at home all the time."

"I'm reaping the benefit today."

"Why did you never learn, Daniel? Did no one ever want to teach you?"

"There's a couple of reasons, I guess. First, my older brother did so well driving the buggy that it was easier to just let him hold the reins. I imagine that if I had ever asked for *Mamm* or *Daed* to teach me, they would've done so." He stopped. Once again, he was embarrassed about his attitude. So much of his life would've been a lot easier if he hadn't had such a big chip on his shoulder.

"But?" she prodded.

He drew a breath. It looked like he was going to have to admit everything after all. "But... I never wanted to do much at home. I was restless and insecure. I hated proving to my father that he was right about me."

She frowned. "Right about what?"

"Right about me not being good at too many things."

"Daniel! What in the world are you talking about?"

Her shock was gratifying, even though he reckoned liking such things said a lot about his ego. "It's nothing you need to worry about, Lela."

"Are you sure?"

"Positive." Unable to help himself, he put an arm around her shoulders and kissed her on the cheek.

She smiled at him. "What was that for?"

"Because I can."

She laughed. Still staring at him, she said, "We should take the courting buggy out again soon."

"Do you really think your parents will allow it?"

She nodded. "My father might not be your biggest fan, but my mother has thawed a bit. *Mamm* knows you make me happy. I think she's almost on my side."

"I hope so." It would be so nice if everything in his life didn't seem like such a battle.

Looking his way again, she scoffed. "I'm sorry, but you need to sound more certain than that. I can't be the only one to be sure that everything is going to work out between us."

"Sorry. I'll try harder." Just as he was about to spout

something about their blooming relationship, he spied an old gray sedan speeding toward them. It was going too fast and seemed to be weaving all over the road.

"Lela! Move to the side."

She looked his way and smiled. "Why?"

"That car is going too fast." When she didn't redirect the horse, he raised his voice. "I'm not joking around. I mean it. Do it now."

"Daniel—Oh, my! You're right." Tensing beside him, she pulled on the right lead. Sable fought for a second, then did as Lela bid. But then, as the car roared closer, the horse whinnied and pulled hard before Lela could try to set the brake.

Daniel couldn't think about anything beyond holding on and wrapping an arm around Lela as Sable started running, mere seconds before the sedan sped past. It was so close, Lela screamed as Daniel stared at the driver's face as he braced for impact.

Only when the vehicle was out of sight did he realize that all three of them—Lela, him and Sable—had survived.

But, boy, were they all shaken up.

Especially since he'd recognized the driver.

Sable, especially, was pulling at the reins. Realizing that Sable was still in danger of taking off—and putting them in further danger—he yelled, "Set the brake, Lela!" He leaped out of the moving buggy and hurried to the horse.

"I just did. Daniel, are you all right?"

"*Jah.* But I don't think the horse is." Sable seemed to be in distress. She was pulling on the reins and looked in danger of hurting herself. The only thing he could think to do was wrap his arms around her neck and try to soothe her. "It's all right, Sable. You're okay."

Again and again, he murmured soothing words, rubbing Sable's head and neck as he did so. She was tense and sweating, but seemed to lean into him a bit. He hoped that was the case and that she was starting to trust him.

After another minute passed, Daniel exhaled, as well, realizing that he felt a little calmer, too.

He was also clutched by a new resolve. Wyatt had been the driver, and there was no doubt about it—he'd come at them on purpose. For some reason, Wyatt had elected not to even swipe the side of the buggy. Perhaps he hadn't wanted to injure Lela and the horse. Or, maybe he'd only wanted to scare all of them? There was no telling.

No matter what, he was pretty sure the worst was over. For that, Daniel knew he'd be giving thanks to God for the next several days.

"Hey, Lela, I think I'm going to stand with her for a few moments. You can just rest in the buggy."

"*Nee*, I don't want to be in this buggy another second." She climbed out and hurried over to them. Tears were running down her face.

He hated to see that.

"Come here." He wrapped one of his arms around Lela's shoulders while he rubbed Sable with his other hand.

Lela snuggled closer, reaching out to rub Sable's shoulder. "You saved the day, Sable," she said. "If you hadn't moved us out of harm's way, all three of us would've been badly hurt."

Sable blew out her breath, no doubt signifying that it had been a very trying day. Daniel agreed whole-heartedly.

"Are you okay? I mean, as well as you can be right this minute?"

"I'm shaken up, but no more than you or the horse." She swallowed. "Daniel, am I losing my mind? For a minute, there, I was sure that car was trying to hit us."

He wasn't going to bring that up because he hadn't wanted to spook her further. But now that she had, he knew he had to give her an honest reply. "You're not losing your mind at all. I thought the very same thing."

"What do you think happened? Was the driver just not paying attention?"

"I could be wrong, but I don't think that was it."

Lela pulled away from him a bit. "What do you think it was?"

Daniel didn't want to tell her. He wasn't sure, and they were standing on the side of the road. The last thing he wanted was to make her more upset than she already was. "Let's talk about it later."

"Are you sure?"

"Yeah." He was about to add more when a pickup truck approached and slowed to a stop just behind them.

The driver got out. It was a man who looked to be in his midforties, wearing a pair of jeans, a blue T-shirt and an unbuttoned flannel over the top of it. "Hey, are you two okay? Some idiot driving a gray sedan just flew by me. He had to be going almost a hundred and was weaving all over the road. I had to slam on my brakes and move to the side. As soon as I saw your buggy I knew I had to stop. Did that guy hurt you or your horse?"

Daniel walked toward him. "We're okay, but I'd appreciate it if you could call someone for me. Would you be able to do that? It's a police detective."

Looking as if he was weighing his words, he said, "You're welcome to use my phone, buddy, but I don't think you need a detective for this. I just called the cops about the driver myself."

"Really? Were you able to give them the car's license plate number?"

"Only three numbers, but I figure someone else is bound to call. Maybe they'll get the rest."

Daniel held out his hand. "I'm sorry, but I think I still do need to use the phone. I'll be quick."

After the man handed his cell phone to him, Daniel punched in Nate's phone number, praising God for giving him the idea to memorize the detective's phone number.

Though he expected to only leave a message, Nate answered. "Hello?"

"Nate, it's me. Daniel. I'm using someone's phone."

"Hey? Are you okay? What's going on?"

"Well, I'm afraid we're in a bit of a situation. I could be wrong, but I'm pretty sure that we were just run off the side of the road." As quickly as he could, Daniel filled Nate in on the courting buggy, their location and his certainty that Wyatt had been behind the wheel.

After pausing for a few moments to write everything down, Nate said, "Any chance you can stay put for a little while? It's going to take me about thirty minutes to get there."

"We can stay, but I don't know if there's much for you to see. We didn't actually get hit."

"I understand, but seeing where he was coming from and heading might help in a small way."

"A man who stopped got part of the license plate number."

"Really? Put him on, okay? I'll be there within thirty minutes. Sit tight."

"I will. Thanks. Here's the phone's owner." Holding it out to the man, Daniel said, "I'm sorry, I never got your name."

"It's Jordan."

"Jordan, thank you for stopping and for letting me use your phone, too. The detective's name is Nate and he wants to speak to you for a moment."

While Jordan began to relay everything he saw, Daniel returned to Lela's side. "I decided to call your uncle, just to let him know what happened. He's on his way out here. I'm sorry, but he asked us to stay."

"I understand." With a frown, she added, "My parents are going to wonder where we are."

"I know." Caught up in the moment, he'd actually forgotten all about her parents—and the fact that they'd finally trusted him enough to take her out for a ride. What a fiasco their outing had turned out to be! First, he could hardly drive a courting buggy, and then they'd almost gotten killed by an out-of-control driver.

Who may or may not have something to do with Brandt's death.

As dates went, he reckoned this one was worse than most. It would be a miracle if Lela ever wanted to see him again.

Chapter Nineteen

Her house looked especially cozy. A fire was burning in the fireplace, a cinnamon-scented candle cast a warm glow in the living room and her mother had put out two of Lela's favorite quilts on the sofa. One had an intricate leaf pattern in shades of brown, red and orange while the other was Lela's great-grandmother's crazy quilt. Each was unique and charming, and each created a warmth in the house that had slowly faded after Brandt had died.

It was really too bad that she wished she was anywhere else.

Sitting on a chair in front of the fireplace, both of her parents were studying her with twin expressions of concern. Though it was usually in her nature to start offering excuses or explanations, she'd stayed quiet. As far as she was concerned, there wasn't a lot she could offer to ease her parents' worries. She was still attempting to understand everything that had happened herself.

In addition, their reactions to everything Uncle Nate had said when he'd dropped her off at home hadn't been all that good. Her mother had cried and her father had tried to blame Daniel. When she had defended Daniel, herself and her uncle, her parents had appeared shocked.

It was only after Uncle Nate had stated for the third time that none of this was anyone's fault but the man who had likely killed Brandt, that her parents had stopped blaming them.

Unfortunately, they now knew that someone was determined to silence Daniel and maybe even Lela, too.

After promising to stop by in a couple of days with an update on the case, her uncle had hugged her tightly and left.

Leaving her to face the consequences by herself.

After a few tense moments passed, her mother spoke.

"Lela, you know we now understand that Daniel isn't as bad as we thought he was. We were wrong to think so badly of him."

It was faint praise, but it was a far cry from the way they'd spoken about him when he'd first returned home. "I do know that."

"He has also been respectful whenever he has been here."

Lela nodded.

After clearing his throat, her father spoke. "I also know he is a hard worker. I've spoken to more than one person who works for Carter and Sons, and they have nothing but praise for Daniel."

She should have known that her father would have asked about Daniel, but it still came as a surprise. "Daniel likes his job there. He says it's a blessing that Mr. Carter gave him a chance."

"It is a blessing," her father said. "His success has

made me wish that I'd listened more and cast fewer stones."

On any other night, Lela knew she would be feeling triumphant. At last, she had found the right man for her and her parents were coming to accept him. Mere weeks ago she had believed that such a thing would never happen.

But at the moment, she was exhausted, emotionally wrung out and half sitting on pins and needles as she waited for her usually direct parents to get to the point. She clenched her hands together in an effort to at least act a little calmer than she was.

Her parents exchanged looks. After her father gave a slight nod, her mother leaned forward. "Lela, even though Daniel is not a bad person, we do not think he's the man for you. You need to stop seeing him."

Even though she'd known the pronouncement had been coming, hearing the words felt like a punch to her stomach. *"Nee."*

Her mother flinched but didn't look away. "I know this isn't what you want to hear, but it's for your own good."

"It is not. I really like him, *Mamm*." She knew she was falling in love with him, but there was no way she was going to share that with her parents! Especially not before she shared her feelings with Daniel.

"Of course you do, but there will be other men. I'm sure the Lord will bring them to you, and you'll understand why He doesn't want you to have a future with Daniel."

Although she truly believed in the Lord working miracles, she did not appreciate her mother's statement.

In fact, it only managed to make her feel even more irritated. "Oh, no. We're not going to pretend that the Lord doesn't want me to love Daniel Miller. It's you who don't want me to see him."

"Lela, you need to control your temper," her father warned.

She'd had enough. Enough sitting, enough defending, enough of everything. She shook her head. "*Nee*. What I need is for you two to understand that I want to be with Daniel. I need him in my life. Just as importantly, he needs me."

Her mother's hands fluttered. "Lela, listen—"

"You listen to me! I was scared tonight. I was afraid for myself and for Daniel. But, what happened made my belief in his innocence even stronger." She lowered her voice. "While you two might believe that the Lord is going to bring another, more suitable man into my life, I beg to disagree. Don't you see? He's already brought a suitable man into my life. After all the odds, all the rumors, all the hate, Daniel still came back here. At first, I didn't even understand it. He was proven innocent. He was given money for restitution. He could've gone anywhere he wanted and started over. But he still came back to our town.

"Don't you think that means something?" she asked as she got to her feet. "Don't you think that there's a reason he came here?"

Standing up as well, her father folded his arms across his chest. "Daughter, you could have died tonight!"

"You're right. I could have. But so could one of you. *Mamm*, you could've slipped and fallen or hit your head. *Daed*, you could've gotten hurt in the barn or chopping wood or even had a heart attack. No one really knows how much time we have on this earth. All we can do is try to be happy and live a life to be proud of."

"Do you really think courting Daniel Miller is that important to you?" her mother asked softly.

"*Jah*. Yes, I do. I truly believe I'm meant to be by his side."

Her mother looked completely torn. "Lela, I fear you are going to make a mistake."

"If I am, it won't be the first time, will it?" Knowing there was nothing else to say, she said, "I love you both but I can't talk about this anymore. I'm exhausted. I'm going to go take a bath and then go to sleep."

Neither of them moved when she walked away.

Giving thanks that she had her own bathroom, Lela pulled a nightgown off the peg on her bedroom wall and hurried into the bath. After turning on the flashlight that always rested on the counter, she turned on the faucet and waited for the stream to warm. When the old-fashioned cast-iron bathtub started to fill, she turned away and looked at herself in the mirror.

Her *kaap* was askew and there was a smudge of dirt on her cheek. Dark shadows had appeared under her eyes, making her look even more tired than she was.

She supposed that shouldn't be a surprise.

Quickly she brushed her teeth and unpinned her dress. Moments later she climbed into the hot water and closed her eyes.

And finally allowed all the events of the evening to fill her thoughts. The concerned driver who lent Daniel his phone. The way Nate had rushed over. The way

Daniel had been more worried about her welfare than his own.

The way she'd been so happy and lighthearted when she'd realized that he couldn't drive a courting buggy too well at all. The way he'd stared at her, like she was everything he'd ever hoped for.

To Lela's surprise, she realized that was what mattered to her the most. That look of adoration that had shone in his eyes for a few precious seconds. He was growing to love her, too.

She wasn't going to give that up. No matter what her parents or anyone else wanted.

There were some things that were worth large sacrifices.

Having Daniel Darrel Miller in her life was one of those things.

Chapter Twenty

The traffic on I71 heading south was backed up for miles. Nate inched along, watching the clock on his dashboard flicker, making his anticipated arrival in Lodi very late. As a pair of cars cut a semi off, he sighed. Years might pass, but some things never changed.

When he'd first joined the police force in Cleveland, he'd been assigned traffic duty, most specifically a stretch of highway on I480, the loop around the city.

Back in those days, he'd taken pride in ticketing out-of-control speeders and anyone who appeared to be driving under the influence of drugs or alcohol. His desk sergeant had enjoyed teasing him about being the rookie class's go-getter. Nate had taken the teasing good-naturedly. After all, he had been proud of doing his job to the best of his ability.

Now that he had several years of service under his belt and had taken the detective exams, he didn't think about monitoring the streets when he was driving. Unless there was an obvious emergency or someone was driving so erratically that they were endangering everyone around him, he didn't do anything.

Sometimes he wasn't sure if that was a good thing or not.

"You've become a little jaded," he told himself as the traffic pattern sped up to thirty-five miles an hour.

Or maybe he was just tired.

Or maybe it was being back in his hometown and among the Amish again. No, he didn't regret jumping the fence, but he was realizing that he'd learned a lot of things about working hard, honesty, loyalty and faith when he'd been growing up. His parents had done a good job with him.

He wished they were still around so he could thank them.

As the traffic slowed again, his phone rang. Seeing that it was his partner, Jill Pavelich, he clicked on the connection. "Hey, buddy," he said. "How's it going?"

"Oh, you know," she drawled, her voice filtering through his SUV's speakers. "I'm dealing with three robberies, an assault, a shooting and two idiot drug dealers."

He grinned. "So, a normal week."

"Yeah. More or less." Sounding grumpier, she added, "It would be a lot better if you were around, Nate. When is that going to happen?"

"You know the answer. When I close this case."

"The lieutenant is really going to let you stay down there indefinitely?"

Boy, she wasn't happy about him being gone so much. "Of course not." He sped up as the traffic eased and started moving at an almost normal pace. "But this is important."

"I know." She sighed. "Believe me, I know."

He knew her well enough to know that she was biting her tongue. "But?"

"But some of the cases I'm dealing with are important, too. I can't be everywhere at the same time."

"Of course you can't."

"You understand, but how can I expect one of the victims to understand, too? I don't even know if they should be expected to think about anything other than the fact that I've promised to help them."

Nate had felt the same thing more than once. Guilt, frustration and lack of time mixed together created a lot of spikes in blood pressure and lack of sleep.

"Even though I'd feel the same way, you know that you have to move some of that load off your shoulders. You're not superwoman," he teased. It was a play on what she always told him—that he wasn't Superman.

"I know, but is it wrong to wish I was?"

He laughed. "Nope. Hey, what's Peck doing?"

"I couldn't tell you."

"Why not? Isn't Sergeant Wilson asking everyone what they're working on during roll call?"

"Yeah, but he's vague. Most of us, even the patrol officers, have learned to give him a wide berth." After a pause, she said, "Rumor has it that the captain is just waiting to get enough evidence to fire Mike."

"Wow. What does the union say?"

"Publicly they're behind him. They have to be, you know?" She continued with barely a pause. "But, I have heard through the grapevine that there's some rumors that, privately, the union rep isn't as gung ho as he acts."

"At least there's that."

"Yeah." Jill paused. "Hey, I just realized I've been pretty unsympathetic to everything you've been going through. Not only are you trying to solve your nephew's murder, but you're back in your hometown and wearing a cop's badge, too. Are you okay?"

Seeing that the exit for Lodi was in two miles, he moved to the right lane. "Yeah. I'm good. It has been hard but it's also made me appreciate some things about my childhood more. I think I've been trying so hard to reinvent myself, I had forgotten that in a lot of ways I'm still the same person. I've been thankful for that blessing."

"Have you spent much time with your family?"

"No. You know both of my parents are gone." He paused as he considered sharing the strain between him and his brother, but decided against it. He doubted Jill would understand the source of the rift, and it was too involved to get into, anyway.

"Well, please know that I might not like you being gone so long, but I feel for you."

"Thanks," he said as he exited. "Listen, I've got to go. I'm finally in Lodi and traffic was so bad I'm already forty minutes late."

"I understand. Good luck and be safe."

"You, too."

Disconnecting, he headed directly to BJ's. It was as good as any place to give the local deputy a call and see if he'd had any luck tracking down Wyatt Troyer's alias.

The deputy answered immediately. He did share that he'd discovered some more information but was due in court. Because of that, he didn't want Nate to stop by until the following day.

Nate was disappointed but didn't push—or point out that he could have left him a message about that this morning instead of waiting until he called.

A knock on his passenger window made him jump.

And then grin.

Opening his door, he smiled at Mitzi as he got out. "Hey, you. This is a nice surprise."

She popped a hand on her hip. "I could say the same thing to you. I was just helping a man get to his car when I realized that it was you in the SUV parked two spaces down. I couldn't resist coming over to say hello."

"I'm glad you did." As always, she looked gorgeous. Today her short red hair fell in wisps around her neck and forehead and her blue eyes were bright. He was tempted to pull her into his arms and lightly kiss her hello, but he knew it was too soon.

They'd only been on one date. And though it had been a good one and there was definitely an attraction between them, no promises had been made.

But that didn't mean that they couldn't spend more time together. Plus, a guy had to eat.

Realizing the wind had picked up and the temperature was lingering around fifty, he closed his door and pressed his key fob to lock the doors. Then he put a hand on the small of her back to guide her inside. "Let's go on in. You look as cute as ever in that old-school uniform, but it's not made for hanging outside in the middle of October. You're going to freeze out here."

She allowed him to guide her in, but seemed wary enough to throw a little bit of attitude. "Nate Borntrager, are you seriously trying to tell me what to do?"

"Not at all. I'm trying to take care of you. At least a little bit."

Her expression softened. "You mean that, don't you?"

"You know I do, Mitzi. You know, if you wanted to trust me a little more, you might be surprised to realize that I'm not going to let you down."

"I might be able to get used to that from time to time."

"I might be real happy if you did," he murmured.

"Nate, I want to trust you, but it's hard for me. You know I was married before and that he wasn't all that nice."

She'd told him about Eric on their date. "I remember. And, if you remember, I told you that I was married years ago, too."

"Well, your separation and divorce might have been amicable but mine was not. Eric stomped on my heart and then stomped on it again when he realized it was still beating."

The picture she was describing broke his own heart. "I don't want to hurt you, Mitzi. I don't even want to try to convince you to trust me until you feel ready. But couldn't you at least try to believe that I have no intention of hurting you on purpose?"

"I want to believe that." Still looking torn, she bit down on her bottom lip. "Nate, if things don't work out between us…"

"Then I'll be disappointed but it'll be okay," he said. "I'm not going to stalk you. I'm not going to try to hurt you or make you miserable."

"Promise?"

"I promise."

She was smiling at him when BJ walked over. "You having lunch with your guy today, Mitzi?"

"Sorry. I'll get back to work."

"No need. Carrie's working today, and we likely won't be real busy for another two hours. Order lunch. It's on me."

Nate grinned. "I'm not even going to hesitate to take you up on that. Thanks. Mitzi, do you know what you want?"

"A veggie burger and sweet potato fries, please."

"Of course. And you, Nate?"

"A double burger, loaded, and a cup of vegetable soup."

"And to drink?"

"I'll get the drinks, BJ. Thanks."

BJ gave her a mock salute as he turned back to the kitchen.

"What would you like to drink?" she asked.

"Water's good."

"You sure?"

"I'm sure, honey. Thank you."

Just as she was about to walk away, she popped a hand back on her hip. "Are you gonna start calling me honey now?"

He laughed. "Well, yeah. After all, I'm your guy now, right?"

Mitzi's eyes widened but she didn't argue. Instead, she walked away to the drink bar.

Giving Nate a moment to feel pleased. The fact that they lived and worked almost two hours away from each other might be difficult. His extended family might not want a lot to do with him. But things were moving forward with Mitzi. He'd take that.

Chapter Twenty-One

The papers had said that there was a good chance of rain that evening, but Lela hadn't let the forecast spoil her mood. For the very first time, she was attending the fall festival with a beau. Getting her parents to agree to the outing hadn't been exactly easy, but Ruth and even her eldest sister, Anna, had stepped in and encouraged their mother and father to give them space.

Though her mother was still rattled by the close call with the out-of-control sedan, even her father had pointed out that rude vehicles passing them wasn't completely uncommon.

Daniel, to his credit, had played a big part in her parents giving in, as well. He'd called on Lela several times, once spending the majority of the evening eating popcorn and working on a puzzle with her and her parents. Lela had thought it would be uncomfortable, but it had been one of their best nights together. Daniel had a way of appreciating even the simplest of things. He'd seemed thrilled to be sipping her mother's homemade hot chocolate and working on a puzzle. When she'd teased him about being so easy to please, he'd flushed, but said there hadn't been a lot of opportunities to do such things when he'd been in prison.

Of course, she'd been embarrassed about her joke and worried that the reminder about his incarceration would upset her parents. But instead of making things worse, it made them better. Both of her parents seemed to treat him more sympathetically after that.

And now, here they were, walking side by side with half of Lodi and looking at all the sights.

Daniel spoke, interrupting her thoughts. "Lela, so far we've looked at the animals, played cornhole, eaten warm pretzels and gone on a hay ride. What would you like to do next?"

"Is there anything more for us to do?" she joked.

He pointed to a wooden sign displaying all the events and their directions. "Oh, *jah*. We could still listen to the band, paint pumpkins, get some more to eat or go in the corn maze."

"What would you like to do?" Daniel had been catering to her wishes the entire time.

"Well, I am hungry. How about we go get some hot dogs and sodas and then venture into the corn maze?"

"Okay." She smiled but feared she didn't sound as enthusiastic as she should. Corn mazes weren't exactly her favorite thing. Since she was so short, the corn towered above her. She was always the last person to figure a way out.

He lightly touched her arm. "What's wrong? We can do whatever you want."

"*Nee*, I want to do that. Let's go eat." They started walking to where about five food trucks were parked in a half circle. Trash cans and picnic tables were arranged in the center.

"There's a lot of other things to eat besides hot dogs..."

"I know. But I like hot dogs just fine. It's..." She gulped. "It's that I get kind of scared in corn mazes. They freak me out."

"Really? I thought you were practically fearless."

She smiled at his comment. "Unfortunately, I'm still scared of corn mazes.

"If you don't like corn mazes, let's avoid this one, okay?"

"You really don't mind?"

"I really don't. I want you happy, not scared." She smiled at him gratefully. "I think my problem with those mazes is that I can't see over the stalks, so I feel too closed in. Almost claustrophobic."

"I'll look out for you, Lela."

"Just promise me that you won't leave me alone."

To her surprise, he stopped right in front of the Burgers and Dogs Food Truck and bent down a few inches so they could look at each other in the eye. "I promise I won't leave you alone in the corn maze."

She realized right then and there that he was being completely serious. He took her worries and fears to heart and was making sure she knew that she was safe with him. Even though she was already halfway to falling in love with him, her insides turned to mush. Daniel really was such a good man. It was a blessing that they'd found each other.

"Okay, let's eat," Daniel said as he guided her to the line. There were only two customers ahead of them. "Look at the menu and tell me what you want."

"One hot dog is enough for me."

"Are you sure? It looks like they have fries and burgers and onion rings, too."

"I'm positive." When it looked like he was about to argue, she shook her head. "Daniel, it's enough. Besides, I'll likely want to get a caramel apple or some hot chocolate after we walk around a little while longer."

He chuckled as they reached the front of the line. "That's a deal. When you get cold, I'll get you a hot chocolate."

"I can pay for that," she volunteered. "I brought money."

"*Nee*, Lela. This whole evening is my treat. It's my honor to take you out."

"Daniel, are you sure? And I'm talking about you paying for everything. Not about it being your honor and all," she clarified with a smile.

"I'm sure about both." Seconds later, it was their turn to order. Daniel ordered two hot dogs and fries for himself and one hot dog for her.

When their food was ready, they went to a picnic table a little off to the side. Some of the other tables were almost full, so it would've been hard to hear each other.

In short order, Daniel ate one of his hot dogs and half of his fries before taking a break. "Sorry, I really was hungry."

She laughed. "No worries." Taking another small bite of her own meal, she pointed to a group of kindergarten-aged children. They were all eating ice cream cones but couldn't seem to stay still long enough to take more than one lick at a time. Consequently, it looked like the treats were going to end up on either their clothes or the ground before they were finished. "I was just looking at those little kids eating ice cream. I hope their mothers have a bunch of napkins."

Looking at where she pointed, Daniel chuckled, too. "You're right. They're going to be a sticky mess." He looked like he was about to add something else, but he suddenly froze. "We need to leave."

"Leave the festival? Why?"

"I think I see Wyatt in that crowd," he said in a low tone. "I'm almost certain of it."

She turned to look but only saw a big crowd near the bandstand. A band was warming up, and there were at least a hundred people milling around, obviously waiting for the music to start. "Do you think he saw us?"

"I'm pretty sure. I felt like he was staring right at me."

A chill raced through her. "Do you have the cell phone that Uncle Nate gave you in case of emergencies?"

He pulled it out. "I do, but I don't want to use it."

"Why not? I think you should call him." She'd heard that her uncle had chastised Daniel for not having it with him when they'd had their frightening episode with the gray sedan.

He slipped it back into his pocket. "I don't think it's a good idea."

"Why not? It's for times like this, right?"

"*Jah*, but I'm still not positive it is Wyatt." He looked around uneasily. "Plus, I don't want to call Nate while we're sitting here, though. There are too many people watching. Someone is bound to notice that an Amish man is chatting on his cell phone and approach us."

Lela didn't really care what people saw or thought, but she didn't argue about that. They had other concerns. "Daniel, I hate to remind you of this, but we're not going to be able to find a ride. We're getting picked up in an hour, remember?"

He closed his eyes. "I'd completely forgotten that."

"I guess we could walk back to my house."

"No way. It's too far and we'll be walking alone in the dark. Anything could happen to us."

Well, that made her feel even more uneasy. "What should we do?"

He was still staring at the crowd surrounding the band, who had just started playing. It was obvious he was weighing the pros and cons of their options.

After another second or two passed, he stood up. "I'm sorry, Lela, but we're going to need to go to the corn maze. I'll have privacy to call your uncle, plus we're going to be able to hide among the stalks if we need to."

"Are you sure?"

"Positive. Come on. We need to hurry."

Quickly, she got up, threw her half-eaten hot dog in the trash and walked by his side.

"We've got to hurry, okay? There's a chance Wyatt won't see where we went if we can get out of here fast."

"Lead the way and I'll follow."

Daniel reached down for her hand, linked their fingers and headed right into a crowd of people surrounding a pair of clowns making balloon animals.

She stayed by his side, practically running as he led them behind a woman selling snacks from a cart and then toward the corn maze.

It looked like she was about to conquer her fear of

corn mazes very soon, since she'd very recently realized that there was something far more frightening than a bunch of really tall cornstalks.

A murderer following them was worse. It was a whole lot worse.

Chapter Twenty-Two

The last time Daniel had spied Wyatt, the other man was grinning at him. It was obvious that he was enjoying this cat and mouse game they were playing, especially now that Lela was involved, as well.

That knowledge gave Daniel chills. He wasn't afraid to defend himself or even fight Wyatt if necessary. But protecting Lela made him scared to death. He didn't know if he was capable of protecting her against someone with so few morals. Daniel had a feeling that nothing was off-limits with the guy—least of all the petite, sheltered woman by his side.

All he knew for sure was that he was going to do his best to try to protect her with everything he had.

After leading Lela through every crowded area he could find, he'd practically thrown five dollars at the corn maze attendant and pulled Lela in.

Daniel wasn't sure if Wyatt had followed them to the corn maze's entrance but it seemed certain that he had or was about to.

After all, Wyatt had nothing to lose. Just two days

ago, Nate had discovered his real name and had sent out an APB, an all-points bulletin, for all local law enforcement personnel. Everyone was now on the lookout for him.

If Wyatt was caught, then Nate would likely ask Daniel to testify against him. Daniel could share his story about seeing Wyatt and Brandt arguing and that it was obvious that Brandt wasn't intimidated by Wyatt one bit. After sharing more information about Wyatt's background that had Mike had never researched, Wyatt would likely go to prison for a very long time. In addition, Lela had already told her uncle that she was willing to go on the witness stand and relay what she'd seen at the farmers market and when they were in the courting buggy.

If Daniel's testimony didn't sway a judge or jury, then seeing Lela on the stand would. After all, she was everything good in the world. Kind and sheltered. Honest and Amish. No jury would ever doubt a single word she said. Even though nothing she could say would link Wyatt to Brandt's murder, Daniel suspected her testimony might help sway a jury against him.

Taking hold of Lela's hand, he pulled her straight ahead and picked up the pace. They needed to get as deep into the corn maze as possible.

Lela stayed by his side, but it was obvious that she was confused. "Daniel, are you sure this is the right way to the end?"

"*Nee*, but I want to get lost. We need to get as hidden as possible as fast as possible."

"Are you sure?"

He hated to see shadows of fear in her expression.

"I'm sorry, but yes. I don't think there are too many other places for anyone to hide around here. Besides, it wasn't like we could sneak our way to the maze. All I could do was try to get here as fast as possible."

"But Daniel—"

"Lela, I know you're scared and I'm real sorry about that. However, we can't stand here and discuss things, okay?" Even though they were still walking, he took care to keep his voice low and gentle. "We need to get farther into this maze. Please, trust me."

"I trust you."

Those three words clutched his heart and held on tight. She was the sweetest person he'd ever met, and the fact that she could give him her trust, too, was almost beyond his dreams. He'd had so many dark days in a prison cell, he'd convinced himself that everything the guards had told him was right. He really was good for nothing and not worth any decent person's time.

Keeping their hands linked, he turned right, then right again, then left. When it felt like they were standing in the very center of the maze, he pulled out his phone. "I think we're finally hidden deep enough in here for me to give Nate a call. We're going to need his help." Still scanning the area, looking for some of the more untended corn rows where they wouldn't be easily seen, he pulled out his phone and clicked on Nate's name.

After one ring, the connection went directly to voice mail.

His blood pressure spiked as his burst of hope plummeted. Why couldn't even contacting Nate be easy? Knowing he had no choice, he spoke quietly into the receiver when the connection buzzed him into voice mail. "Nate, it's Daniel. Me and Lela need you. We're at the fall festival on the edge of town. I saw Wyatt and I'm pretty sure he saw us. I didn't know what else to do, so I brought Lela into the corn maze. It's real big and overgrown. I think it's our only hope of staying hidden. I'll try to stay there with Lela for as long as we can. Call me." Just as he took a breath to tell Nate that Wyatt was wearing a blue shirt, the connection ended.

Daniel's heart sank. He wasn't even positive that the detective had received his message. He stared at the screen of his phone in dismay. What was he going to do if Nate didn't get the message?

Desperate, he called 911. The moment the operator answered, he blurted his name, where he was, and that he needed Nate's help. Too scared to stay on the line, he hung up.

Lela moved closer. "Do you think anyone is going to help us?"

"I don't know. Nate didn't answer and I didn't want to stay on the line when I called 911."

"Maybe…"

"*Nee.* We canna stop to talk." As his panic overtook him, he reached for her hand and tugged.

But instead of complying, she tugged on his shirt. "Daniel, stop for a second."

Daniel knew he was scaring her and regretted that. He really did. However, he would regret it even more if she got hurt. "We canna stop," he replied through gritted teeth. "We need to keep going."

"*Nee*, we need to be smart about this. If he's in this maze, we need to hide, not keep wandering around.

Or, better yet, we should get out of here. We can walk home. I know you don't want us to walk alone in the dark, but I bet we'll be all right."

He wished it could be that easy. But if they walked away it would make them even more isolated and vulnerable. "I'm too afraid to do that, Lela. I can't risk you getting hurt. At least here we'll be surrounded by people. And, if Nate did receive our message, he knows where to look for us."

"But if we're hiding, that won't matter."

"We can run out in the open. Or yell for people to help." It wasn't a good option, but it was better than nothing.

He could practically feel her dismay.

Leading her down another path, Daniel winced, hating how that didn't sound very smart, either. But what could he do? "Lela, I wish I had a better plan, but I'm making this up as we go along."

"All right." She pointed to a spot where they could turn right. "Let's go this way."

"Are you sure?"

"Trust me, Daniel. I may not like mazes, but I'm sure that I've been in more than you have. Plus I have an idea."

Though part of him wanted her to do nothing but trust him, he knew that wasn't a good idea. Lela was smart and she was tougher than she looked. "All right, but if I tell you to run without me, do it."

"Why would you think I'd do that? Do you think I'd just leave you if you were in danger?"

"You better."

"*Nee.*"

"I don't want to argue with you, Lela."

"Then stop saying stupid stuff. I might not have been in prison or done any of the things you did during your *rumspringa*, but I'm not stupid. I'm well aware of the danger we're in. Trust me, Daniel."

There was that word again. Trust. Of course, he'd just asked her to trust him, but he honestly didn't know if he trusted anyone or anything anymore. Not the justice system, not friends, not even his parents a hundred percent. He reckoned most people would find it harder to love, but he had no problem loving. He loved his family and his brother and sisters, even though he didn't trust them to have his back. He was falling in love with Lela. But did he trust her judgment to keep them safe?

Probably as much as his own.

"I trust you," he said at last.

Her eyes shone. "Let's go, then."

This time, Lela led the way and he followed. To his surprise, the switch in roles helped him refocus. He was able to keep his eyes peeled for any signs of Wyatt. Just as he had turned around to make sure no one was following, Lela drew to a stop.

"Oh!"

He turned and saw what had her looking so nervous. In front of them were five children and two mothers. It was obvious that the children couldn't decide whether to turn right or left, but the mothers were letting them make the decision. No doubt Lela was thinking the same thing that he was—that all innocent bystanders needed to get out of their way.

Daniel was very tempted to encourage the group to move on, preferably far from him and Lela, but he didn't dare. After nodding politely at the mothers, he turned to Lela. "Which way?"

"Right." She waved at the children. "Have a good night."

"Bye!" a particularly cute boy with red hair called out.

After they turned, it seemed to be more and more crowded. There were groups of teenagers, arguing about which way to go. There were families with their *kinner*, the parents appearing rather fed up with the maze.

And then, of course, there were the inevitable couples seeking privacy and seclusion. Each time they got close, the boys would scowl at them.

The third time that happened, Lela giggled softly. "Those boys are acting like we've got nothing better to do than spy on them."

He smiled at her. "I was thinking the same thing. Imagine what would happen if we were hiding where one of the couples stopped to kiss?"

"We'd probably scare them half to death."

"Likely so."

Lela turned left again and breathed a sigh of relief when no one was in sight. "I can't be sure, but I think we're close to the end of the maze, Daniel. I think we should hide around here."

He noticed that this area, unlike most of the other paths, wasn't lit by a battery-powered lamp. Instead, it was a dark tunnel filled with just the faintest of shadows. "I think you're right. Come on. Let's go in and hide among the cornstalks."

"Great." Her voice was fairly dripping in sarcasm.

"What's wrong? Do you think we should do something else?" he said in a whisper.

"Not at all. I just don't want to stand in the midst of all those stalks."

"Because you get claustrophobic?"

"Yes, and all the bugs. These cornstalks are going to be riddled with bugs and rodents. I hope nothing crawls up my dress."

If they were anywhere else he would be tempted to tease her. Well, maybe he should, anyway. "We're on the run and you're worried about bugs? I didn't know you were so squeamish."

"Sorry, but I am."

"Even though you're a pet sitter?"

"Watching furry animals ain't the same thing as being nestled among a bunch of grasshoppers."

Standing in the middle of the path, he spotted a good clump of cornstalks. Getting in the middle of them wouldn't be easy, but he was almost certain that they would be sufficiently hidden. "Come on, scaredy-pants."

To Lela's credit, she didn't say much in response. She simply followed him into hiding. It took a moment—and Lela was right, there were bugs—but in no time at all, they were nestled in among the stalks. With Lela in her dark blue dress and him in his dark pants, gray shirt and black hat, he was confident that they were as hidden as they could hope to be.

Except for her pristine white prayer *kapp*.

"Lela, do you have your bonnet?"

"Why?" she whispered.

"Your *kaap* is going to be gleaming in the moonlight."

"I don't think I can take it off easily. Can you reach it?"

"I think so. Do you want me to remove it?"

"Please."

"Are you sure?" For some reason, he felt that asking her to do such a thing was worse than asking her to remove her dress.

"I'm sure. God will understand."

Realizing that he felt the same way, he did as she asked and carefully removed the prayer covering. "I'll, ah, just fold it and slip it in my pants' pocket."

"Okay."

They stood in silence for several minutes. Daniel heard chatter and laughter floating through the stalks, but no one close.

Actually, standing there so still in the dark, surrounded by cornstalks and the elements and a slight hint of cool air, Daniel seemed to be only aware of one thing: Lela. Lela was standing so close that he could feel her warm breath against his throat.

No, it was more than that. He was aware of every single thing about her. The worn, soft fabric of her dress. The light scent of lavender and jasmine. He wondered if it came from her shampoo or body lotion. The way she was standing so close yet it didn't feel uncomfortable. No, it felt right. Almost like they were meant to be together.

Almost like she was his reward for surviving years behind bars. The agonizing confusion when he'd first realized that no one was going to come forward to his defense during the trial. That it really was possible to be arrested, charged and ultimately convicted of a crime that he hadn't done.

Returning to his home and his hometown—and realizing that the truth still didn't matter. At least not the truth that he saw. He'd been found guilty again, not because he'd fired a gun but because of his character.

And he hadn't been able to deny that conviction.

But now, here he was, practically holding a beautiful girl in the evening. He was breathing not just her scent but also fresh air. Both things were gifts he'd never let himself think about. They were too unattainable. But now, here he was.

He swallowed. He knew he should be ashamed. Lela Borntrager was sweet and good. He shouldn't be thinking about her in such a personal way. He shouldn't be allowing himself to imagine that there would be anything between them when this was all over but regrets. His own regret for pulling her into his life and her regret for ever giving him the time of day.

She clasped his arm, pulling him out of the reverie. "Lela?" he whispered.

When she swayed toward him, he reached out and curved his hands around her waist. "What's wrong?"

"I…"

She was about to faint. "Your knees are locked, sweetheart," he murmured. "Take a deep breath and bend your knees. I've got you."

He knew she looked up at him and wished he could look into her eyes.

"You called me sweetheart."

"I—" He stopped, hearing footsteps approaching.

His hands still on her waist, he squeezed slightly, hoping she would understand his signal.

She did, because she tensed up again.

As the footsteps drew closer, he said a prayer. Giving thanks that she was staying quiet. Asking for the Lord's protecting hand. Praying that Nate was on his way. And, hoping against hope that Lela wouldn't faint on him now.

Chapter Twenty-Three

It had taken Nate two weeks of phone calls, numerous texts, a dozen promises and four more meals at BJ's to persuade Mitzi to let him take her out to dinner for a second time.

He supposed he didn't blame her reticence. The first time they'd met, at a quaint bistro in the nearby town of Medina, things hadn't gone all that well. His phone had kept beeping with work-related messages about another case that was about to go to trial. Since the texts were from an assistant district attorney and his lieutenant, he hadn't felt like he could ignore either.

Little by little, he'd watched some of Mitzi's appreciation for their date dwindle. He hadn't blamed her, which made it even harder to keep answering the texts. Only because a man's life was at stake had he continued to respond. That was more important than his love life—or lack of one.

That said, even after they'd said good-night and their subsequent conversations had been strained, he'd pressed on. He might not deserve Mitzi's time, but he still craved it.

After his fourth meal at BJ's, she'd agreed to give him another chance.

To Nate's amusement, instead of allowing him to take her someplace fancy for a steak dinner or a romantic spot for Italian, she'd wanted to go to a nearby Amish restaurant.

That's why they were sitting in a very family-friendly restaurant eating broasted chicken, mashed potatoes with gravy and squash casserole while being surrounded by far too many restless kids. It was impossible to ignore their complaints or their parents' admonishments.

He, personally, liked broasted chicken as much as anyone, but the atmosphere was nothing like the way he'd planned to sweep her off her feet.

Mitzi, who'd been very much enjoying her own plate of chicken, put down her fork. "Uh-oh. You're frowning."

"Am I? Sorry."

"What's wrong? Do you not like your meal?"

"I like it fine." He smiled at her. "Who doesn't like Amish-prepared chicken?"

She still looked concerned. "If it's not the food, then what is on your mind?"

And...now he felt worse—and frustrated with himself. He'd been trying to get this date for weeks and what happened? He couldn't even be a good conversationalist when it counted. "It's nothing. I promise. I... I guess my mind was drifting."

She still hadn't picked back up her fork. "Are you thinking about work?"

"No. Absolutely not."

That was actually something he'd promised not to do if she consented to go out with him a second time. During one of their recent phone conversations, she'd revealed that her ex-husband had constantly been staring at his phone whenever they went out or spent time together. She'd shared that she'd hated feeling like she always came in second place, to his work but also his friends, sports scores, even Instagram posts.

Realizing that he'd inadvertently made her feel the same way, he'd swallowed his pride, called his lieutenant and said he'd needed four hours off the clock. Nate didn't know if he felt relieved or embarrassed that his boss had agreed to his request immediately. Obviously, he should've asked for the same grace before their first date.

Noticing that Mitzi didn't look all that convinced—and who could blame her?—he attempted to explain himself. "Please eat. I was…well, at the risk of sounding like a complete jerk, I was thinking that this place isn't what I had in mind when I was attempting to convince you to go out with me again."

He tensed, pretty much waiting for her to roll her eyes or tease him.

But instead, her whole posture relaxed. "You are too funny. I know I seemed annoyed during our first date, but I realized I overreacted."

"You were justified."

"I might have been justified in wanting all your attention, but you answering two important people about a man's upcoming trial is a lot different than wishing Eric would stop looking at basketball scores on his phone."

He smiled at her. "I appreciate that, but you were

right. I called my lieutenant and asked for four hours off the clock. He agreed."

Her whole expression softened. "I can't believe you did that. That is so sweet. You are so sweet, Nate."

Pleased that she'd picked back up her fork, he grinned. "You might be the first person in my entire life to ever say that about me."

"If that's the case, it's about time, then."

Glad the tension between them had relaxed again, he said, "Now, I have something important to ask."

"Yes?"

"What kind of pie are you going to order?"

She laughed. "There's too many to choose from, but I'm leaning toward coconut cream pie. What about you?"

"I might go big and do something different, like butterscotch or peanut butter."

"Living dangerously, I see."

"You only live once," he joked, then frowned when he noticed his phone was vibrating, signaling an incoming call.

"Is that your phone?"

"It is, but don't worry. Like I said, I requested a few hours off. I deserve that." He shook his head slightly. "No, I mean we deserve it."

To his surprise, though, she didn't look all that relieved. "Could it be work?"

"Yes, but it can wait. I'm off."

"Okay."

He sipped from his water and was just about to put his phone in his jacket when it buzzed again. Warning signals rang in his ears. Everyone at work had been notified to give him some space. It had actually been a source of amusement for the dispatcher, who'd teased him about falling in love.

With effort, he ignored it again.

"Nate, if you need to get that—"

"Nope. I was sincere when I promised you that I wouldn't be on my phone, Mitzi."

Instead of looking relieved, she appeared even more torn. "Like I told you before, I think I was being unfair. I don't think criminals only commit crimes when you're on duty."

"You're right, but I'm not the only detective at the station. They'll handle it."

Of course, his phone started vibrating for a third time, instantly followed by two text messages. He frowned at it again, but his hand itched to see what was going on. Though the captain encouraged all employees to honor time off, emergencies happened.

But what if he lost this woman because he couldn't even give her four simple hours?

"I think you'd better at least see what's happening," Mitzi said quietly. "I'm serious, Nate."

As much as he wanted to hold steady to his promise, he knew what he had to do. Only something really urgent would have brought so many phone calls and texts.

Besides, if he and Mitzi did have a future, she'd have to know what being a cop's girlfriend or wife meant.

"I am sorry," he said before swiping his phone.

There were two text messages from his lieutenant.

"Nate, can you get there?"

The second message was more urgent.

"Where are you? I'm sending a car there now."

Almost forgetting where he was, he clicked the voice mail. When he heard Daniel's voice, his stomach dropped. His worst fears had materialized. Even though they'd had officers scouring the area, they still hadn't done a good enough job. He'd failed Daniel. Even worse, he'd put Lela in danger. If something happened to her, he'd never be able to forgive himself. The next two messages were from both the dispatcher and his lieutenant.

He stood up. He should've been there ten minutes ago. "Mitzi, I'm so sorry but I've got to go." Pulling out his wallet, he threw some bills on the table.

She stood up, as well. "What happened? Can you tell me?"

He was relieved she looked concerned and not irritated with him. "Daniel and my niece are in trouble." Though he didn't usually share anything about his cases, he couldn't help himself. "I'm afraid they're in danger."

She paled. "You're referring to Lela, aren't you?"

He nodded as he texted the officers to let them know he was on his way.

Sliding out of the booth, she grabbed her purse. "I'll come with you."

He shook his head. "You don't understand. I wasn't exaggerating. This… It's dangerous, Mitzi."

She started walking to the door. "First of all, you picked me up, so you're my ride. Secondly, I know her. I know Daniel, too. I'm emotionally involved. I want to help."

He was in too much of a hurry to stand and argue

with her. "Look. I'm sorry, but you're going to have to call for an Uber or something. This is—"

"I'll stay in the car. I'll stay out of the way. I'll do whatever you need me to do. But I'm going with you. When you save them, those kids are going to be scared to death. You're going to be busy. I can be the helping hand. Trust me."

He might be making a huge mistake, but he didn't think so. "All right."

He punched in his Lieutenant's number, but it went straight to voice mail. In short order, he filled in his lieutenant about the location and the time he expected to arrive.

After debating for a moment about whether to call someone else, Nate clicked his key fob to unlock his car. Mitzi got in.

While he stood there, fighting back the urge to change his mind or lecture her about safety, she called out, "We don't have time for this, Nate. Get in and let's go. Time's a wasting."

Hoping and praying that he wasn't about to put her in danger, Nate got in on the driver's side, started the car and pulled out of the parking lot. "You better mean what you said. You have to stay out of the way. They're in danger. You could be in danger."

Her reply was immediate. "That means you could be in danger, too, big guy."

Unbelievably, he almost smiled. "Big guy?"

"It fits you. You're tall, all muscles and have the biggest heart of any man I've ever known. As far as I'm concerned, you're amazing."

Her words made him choke up as he sped along the

highway. "I can't deal with this now." They made his insides soften and his mind stray to a future with her. A future where they could be there for each other.

"You don't need to deal with anything but Daniel and Lela."

"You're something else, Mitzi. I don't deserve you."

"Sure you do." Her voice softened. "Nate, don't you understand? I'm already halfway in love with you."

"Mitzi." She was killing him.

"You don't need to say a word. Just let me talk. I'm falling for you for a whole bunch of reasons, and none of them have to do with you being a cop."

"Or because I ruined our first night out?"

"You didn't ruin it. You made me realize just how much you care. Nate, when I look at you, I see a man who has a soft spot for kids who need a hero. I see someone who cares so much, you risk hurting yourself in order to do what's right."

"I'm not a hero."

"You are to me. I want to be with you."

"When we get there, stay in the car. I mean it."

"I promised that I would."

As he turned left and pulled into the festival's unpaved parking lot, he nodded.

But in his mind he was thinking about how he'd promised to stay off his phone and he'd done it, anyway. Some promises, it seemed, were meant to be broken.

Man, he hoped her promise wasn't one of those. If she got hurt, he would never forgive himself.

Chapter Twenty-Four

Lela was really cold. So cold, she was shivering and her hands felt like icicles. She couldn't understand why that was, though. The temperature was on the cool side, but not that cold—likely not much below fifty degrees. She was also dressed warmly. She had on a wool dress, thick stockings and boots. She even had on some very cute fingerless gloves that Ruth had given her last year for Christmas. In addition, she was wedged in the middle of some very uncomfortable cornstalks. She would have never imagined that they could act as insulation. So, she should be rather cozy.

And then there was the fact that she was standing right next to Daniel. Thinking about it, she decided that description didn't exactly do their positions much justice. She wasn't just standing next to him, her body was practically flush with his own. He was also radiating heat. She should feel like she was standing next to a furnace.

Nothing could be further from the truth.

Her entire body was trembling, and her hands were so chilly she was clenching them in tight fists.

Knowing that she needed to stand still and stay quiet, she decided to close her eyes and pretend she was some-place else. In front of the fireplace at home. Walking in the fields near the house in the middle of summer.

Neither helped. She shivered again.

Daniel noticed. Keeping his voice low, he spoke into her ear. "Lela, are you okay?"

"Jah."

"You're trembling. Are you that scared?"

"Nee. I'm cold." Of course, she was scared to death, too, but she didn't want to make things worse.

"Really?"

She nodded. "I don't know why."

After a few seconds' pause, he whispered again. "I do. You're frightened."

She half hoped he'd spout a bunch of words about how everything was going to be okay. How they both were going to be all right because their hiding place was fantastic.

It seemed he wasn't going to sugarcoat things for her. She supposed that was good. When her body shivered again, Lela reckoned her muscles, like her brain, were wishing he'd be a little more optimistic.

They stayed quiet for several minutes. The light breeze brushed against the cornstalks, causing them to rustle and sway. After perhaps ten minutes passed, Daniel cocked his head to one side, seemed to listen for footsteps and then shifted positions. He wrapped his arms around her, somehow managing to pull her even closer. She was so surprised by the embrace, she froze. What was she supposed to do now?

"Hey, don't be scared," he murmured. One of his hands lightly rubbed her back. "It's okay. Just lean into me. *Jah?* I'll keep you warm and safe."

They were sweet words. Maybe they were even the assurances she'd been craving. Unfortunately, they didn't calm her down.

After all, they both knew that he really couldn't keep her safe, not really. Not if Wyatt had a gun.

However, since the alternative was to disagree, she did the only thing that she could. Lela nodded and allowed her face to rest against his chest. Closing her eyes, she heard the faint beating of his heart. It was steady and sure.

At last, she found comfort.

Daniel didn't speak again. Instead, he slowly ran his hand along her spine. Again and again, his warm skin traced the ridges of her spinal column and soothed.

Lela wished she could help him in some way. No doubt Daniel was as worried as she was. It would be a good thing for her to utter something positive. Something to let him know that she believed in him, and that she was sure they were going to be just fine. Instead, all she was able to do was cry. Tears welled in her eyes and slowly fell. No doubt she was making his shirt wet.

She hoped he didn't notice.

But of course Daniel did. He moved his hands again, this time simply holding her in a close embrace. "I know," he whispered. *"I know."*

Just as Lela was about to sniff, she heard footsteps again. This time, the footsteps were far slower than the other people who had passed them. Every two or three steps, they stopped. Cornstalks rustled.

Daniel squeezed her waist, a nonverbal reminder that they needed to be completely silent and motionless.

She knew that it had to be Wyatt and he was looking for them. The tears fell faster, and her stupid nose started to drip. In any other situation she would've been embarrassed.

Now she just hoped she wouldn't get dizzy again and faint.

Closing her eyes, she began to pray. She prayed for help. Prayed for Nate. Prayed for her family, just in case she and Daniel didn't make it out of the cornstalks alive.

She prayed as hard as she ever had in her life.

She knew the Lord was really busy. There were likely floods and fires and all kinds of terrible things happening everywhere in their flawed world. And yet, she couldn't help but hope that there was a part of Him that could feel her need and would answer her prayers.

She hoped and prayed with all her might.

The footsteps drew closer. The cornstalks rustled again, this time only about six feet away. Wyatt was going to find them.

She bit her lip to keep from crying out.

Holding Lela in his arms, a thousand emotions warred in Daniel's head. Dismay that the Lord couldn't even give him one easy night with Lela. Anger that the police, despite all of their promises, still couldn't pin down Wyatt. Hope that Nate or anyone had gotten his message and was coming to the rescue.

But most of all, he felt guilty. He should've known

that Wyatt was no doubt waiting for the perfect opportunity to finally make his move. He should've been smarter.

No, he should've done a hundred things instead of bringing Lela into so much danger.

"Daniel, I know you're here," Wyatt called out in a singsong voice.

Daniel wasn't sure if Wyatt was on the path right next to them or several paths over. Between the wind and the rustling cornstalks, it was hard to gauge distance.

Lela shivered again. He slowly edged his arms tighter around her, silently urging her not to move. Not even an inch.

Whether she didn't get the signal or couldn't help herself, she shivered again.

Then one of her feet moved to the side. The movement caused a cornstalk to rustle more loudly than before.

He didn't blame Lela, but boy did he wish she hadn't done that.

Loud footsteps came closer. "Daniel, is that you? Who are you here with? That pretty girl you're always staring at?"

Wyatt's voice was more confident. He was going to find them, kill Daniel and then be alone with Lela.

He stopped hoping and praying and started mentally planning what he was going to do when Wyatt reached where they were.

But instead of walking closer, Wyatt moved a little farther away. Through a tiny gap in the cornstalks, Daniel could see he had on a light-colored shirt. It reflected against the moonlight and fairly glowed. At least he wasn't blending into the dark, Daniel supposed.

A crow cawed overhead, breaking the silence.

More birds cawed, followed by the squeals and laughter of some teenagers.

A gust of wind passed through the field, causing all the stalks to rustle in response.

Across the walkway, Wyatt's movements became more intense. Forceful. Daniel could hear his hands reaching into the dried cornstalks.

"You know, you've been harder to fool this time around," Wyatt continued. Almost conversationally.

He laughed softly. "I guess spending all that time around criminals taught you a thing or two, huh? Good for you. At least something good happened in prison, right?"

Daniel closed his eyes, reminding himself that Wyatt was a grifter, a drug dealer and a liar. He was going to say whatever he could in order to get a rise out of Daniel or to make Lela so upset that she would move or cry out.

Daniel wished he could say something encouraging to Lela. He wished there was anything he could do to ease her fears. Of course he wasn't going to say a word.

Besides, what did he actually have that could be of use? Only two arms to hold her close and a will to fight Wyatt in order to protect her.

Wyatt was still on the other side of the walkway, combing through the cornstalks.

"You know, what's really sad is that you brought that girl into this," he said, once again speaking like they were sipping coffee in front of a fireplace. His voice darkened. "But bringing her here is on you, Daniel. You know that, right? It's not my fault that you brought her. You should've left her alone. I don't want to hurt her. I really don't. But you've given me no choice, right? Whatever happens isn't my fault."

When a crow cawed again, this time just behind Daniel and Lela, his heart sank.

Sure enough, Wyatt stepped closer. Lela inhaled and held her breath. If they weren't in such danger, Daniel would've reminded her to exhale. To breathe.

The cornstalks parted just four feet away. Then three.

Then, just when Daniel thought the wait couldn't be any more excruciating, the stalks that had shielded them so well for so long broke apart.

Suddenly, they were looking into Wyatt's eyes.

Reflected by the light shirt and the full moon, Wyatt's expression was full of triumph.

He chuckled. "I knew I would find you. I knew it. And, you, Lela Borntrager, are my prize for not giving up. We're going to have a great time together. I just know it." He reached out and brushed a strand of hair from her face.

Lela cried out.

"Don't touch her." Daniel stepped forward and pushed her behind him. "She's not who you want. She's not who you've been after. You'll have to kill me first."

"Nee!" Lela said.

Grinning, Wyatt pulled out a gun.

Chapter Twenty-Five

Wyatt looked exactly like he had in the farmers market. His hair was still a little too long and dark red, and he wore a scruffy beard. In addition, he had on a cream-colored flannel shirt and dark work pants. He was tall and looked so mean. His eyes fairly glinted with something dark and disturbing.

Lela knew that Daniel would do everything he could to save her but that it wasn't going to be enough. He was going to need help, and the only person to provide that help was her.

She was small and slight, though. There was no way she was ever going to be able to fight him.

But...she did have a very loud scream. Everyone in her family had always commented on it.

Drawing in her lungs, Lela screamed with all her might. "*Nee!* Don't shoot!" She screamed again, this time calling for help as loud as she could.

As if he hadn't expected her to say a single word, Wyatt took a step backward. "Shut up! Stop yelling!"

No way was she going to be quiet. Inhaling, she screamed again. "Help! Someone help!"

"Get her quiet, Daniel," Wyatt warned.

"Or what?" he asked. As if he had nothing to lose! Lela felt like kicking his shin.

She opened her mouth to scream again, and a distant voice called out, "Where are you?"

"Here! In the maze! Help us, please!" she yelled before Wyatt covered her mouth with his hand.

She pushed at him, but he jerked her so hard, she felt as if her body was as limp as one of the scarecrows standing at the front of the maze.

Panicking, she struggled again.

"Stop fighting me. You're not going to win," Wyatt said. "I've got you."

"No, you don't," Daniel said under his breath seconds before he slammed his fist into Wyatt's jaw.

The force was strong enough that Wyatt released Lela.

"Run, Lela," Daniel said, still not taking his eyes off of Wyatt.

There was no way she was going to run. She was going to stay by his side no matter what happened. Lela took care to stay motionless as Wyatt swung at Daniel. He easily avoided the contact and then hit Wyatt again.

His head jerked back from the impact. Then he frowned as blood started to pour out his nose. "You broke my nose."

He sounded surprised. No, shocked.

"What do you think happened to me in prison?" Daniel asked in a sarcastic tone. "Did you really think that I didn't learn how to defend myself during all that time?"

Wyatt curled a lip. "I didn't think you would've survived the first night. You were so weak. So needy." He grinned. "So easily influenced. Blame me for all your problems if you want, but you and I both know I didn't have to con you into going to parties or getting buzzed. You were always up for that."

"You knew I didn't kill anyone."

"*Of course* you didn't. You couldn't shoot a dog in a cage. I shot Brandt. The moment I asked if he wanted to start dealing, he turned on me. He was going to go to the cops."

"I was innocent."

"No, *you were convenient.* I knew you would be too scared to defend yourself. I knew you were the perfect person to pin this on the moment you held the gun."

"You offered it to me. Said I might want to know what holding it felt like. I wouldn't have touched it otherwise."

His brown eyes glinted. "Yeah, I said that, all right." He swiped at his nose with the side of his hand. "I was going to do whatever it took to make sure you took the fall."

"You're going to pay for that. If it's the last thing I ever do, I'm going to make sure you go to prison for Brandt's death and for framing me."

"I'm not going anywhere because I won't have any witnesses."

"That's not going to happen. Any fight we're in. I'll win. You're strung out and weak."

Just as Wyatt lunged for him, her uncle Nate and another officer appeared at the end of the row.

"Uncle Nate!"

Though Nate wasn't looking directly at her, his body signified that he was very relieved. "Lela, thank the Lord."

Immediately Wyatt turned on his heel and pointed the gun at the first officer.

Without hesitating, the police officer raised his own pistol and pointed it at Wyatt. "Don't try it," he said. "I shoot to kill."

Wyatt blinked, lowered his gun for a few moments, then seemed to collect himself again. His eyes turned even more crazed as he pointed the gun at her uncle, then Daniel, then her. Lela gasped.

"Hold it!" Nate yelled. His gun was drawn and he was staring intently at Wyatt. "Don't do it, son."

"I'm not your son."

"No, you aren't. But you're not my enemy, either. Don't make this any worse than it already is. I promise, if you hurt my niece, you won't see the light of day."

"I…"

"Put the gun down."

When Wyatt hesitated again, Daniel suddenly swung his right hand at the back of Wyatt's head. He went down like a ton of bricks.

Moments later, Wyatt came to. But by that time Nate had already cuffed him.

When he started to read Wyatt his rights, Daniel walked to Lela's side.

"How are you holding up?" he whispered.

"I don't know," she said. "I feel shaky and kind of weak." She shrugged. "Part of me can't believe that any of this happened. I feel like I was in the middle of a movie or something."

"I wish it had been, but your uncle saved the day."

"So did you," she said as he took her into his arms. "You fought him and were winning."

"Lela, you helped, too," her uncle said, as two other officers joined them and escorted Wyatt away. "People heard your screams and not only kept calling 911 but also directed us about where to go."

"Really?"

"For sure. I wouldn't lie about that."

She giggled. "I would've never guessed that screaming my head off would be helpful."

"Let's not make a habit of this, okay?"

Looking into Daniel's eyes, she shook her head. "I'm fine with that."

"Now what happens?" Daniel asked Nate.

"I know out here is the last place you want to be, but I'm afraid we're going to need the two of you to stick around. We're going to ask you a ton of questions."

Daniel nodded. "I understand, but it's gotten pretty cold, and we've been out here a long time. Could maybe someone get Lela a blanket or something?"

Nate suddenly smiled. "I can do better than that." Pulling out his phone, he texted something. After a second's wait, he smiled. "Someone is going to join us and bring both blankets and some cups of hot coffee."

Lela was shocked. "The police carry coffee in their patrol cars?"

"*Nee.* We have blankets, but Mitzi is doing the rest," Nate replied with a smile.

"Wait, Mitzi from BJ's Burgers?"

Looking almost bashful, her uncle nodded. "Yes. We were out on a date tonight when I received word about what was going on with you two. When I apologized because I had to leave, Mitzi insisted on coming with me. The only way I would let her come was if she promised to stay in the car. She's going to be thrilled to do something useful."

"It sounds like Daniel and I weren't the only ones to have an interesting night," Lela said.

Nate winked. "You're right about that. Next time all of us go out, though, let's keep things a whole lot quieter."

"Amen to that," Daniel said.

Privately, Lela said that, as well. She would be very happy to be surrounded by a lot of peace and quiet from now on. She would also be extremely happy if she was never near another cornstalk for the rest of her life.

Chapter Twenty-Six

After the police arrived and Wyatt—also known as Joey Stanton—had been arrested and taken into custody, the rest of the night became a blur.

Daniel remembered staying close to Lela, sipping coffee and constantly checking to make sure that she was warm enough nestled under the blanket.

As the minutes passed, Lela seemed to collect herself. She hugged Mitzi and her uncle, answered the officers' questions, and even giggled once when one of the uniformed policemen jumped back from a cornstalk, saying that the thing was riddled with giant stink bugs.

After another hour at the scene, one officer drove him home while Mitzi and Nate took Lela back to her house. Daniel had hated to be separated from her. Not only was he still worried about her being scared and in shock, he couldn't shake his guilt—or his regret. He was fairly sure that her parents were never going to allow him within ten feet of her. He didn't blame them, either. Everything that had happened was because of his stupidity and arrogance. Even though he loved her with everything he had, she deserved someone far better than himself.

He hadn't thought he'd be able to sleep, but after getting home and taking a hot shower, he collapsed in his apartment and barely moved for eight hours.

When he woke up a little after nine in the morning, he learned that the almost shoot-out and the arrest of Brandt's real killer had made the evening news and the morning's paper.

Abraham knocked on Daniel's door soon after he'd drunk his first cup of coffee. His friend looked very pleased to let him know that Craig had given Daniel the day off—with pay.

When Daniel invited him in for a cup of coffee, Abraham was filled with questions about the evening's events. Daniel had thought he wouldn't want to talk about hiding in the maze and his fight with Wyatt, but sharing what happened—and how scared he'd been—had actually helped.

Getting it out in the open reminded him to not be so hard on himself. Everything that had happened had been far beyond any of their wildest imaginings. How could he have guessed that Wyatt had been watching them for days and had purposely picked the perfect place to track them down?

When he finished his story, Abraham's eyes were as big as saucers. "That's some kind of story."

"I reckon it is."

"You're a hero, man. I'm proud of you."

"There's nothing to be proud about. If the police hadn't arrived at the right moment, Wyatt would've shot me and probably taken Lela hostage." Just imagining what could've happened, he swallowed. "Or something worse."

"*Jah*, the Lord did bring the police in the nick of time, but you and Lela thought fast on your feet." Abraham grinned. "And it sounds as if you have a mighty *gut* right hook!"

"You know violence is nothing to be proud of."

His buddy rolled his eyes. "Of course not...unless it meant that you protected both yourself and your girlfriend." After taking another fortifying sip of coffee, he whistled low. "I have to tell ya, Daniel, I didn't know you had that in ya. I would've stood there like a scared-to-death fool."

"I don't think you would have. The Lord was with me and helped me do things that I didn't think I could." He had a feeling he'd be saying prayers of thanks for the rest of his life.

Abraham turned and looked out the window. "Hmm. It looks like you've got company. A vehicle just pulled up."

He groaned. "Who is it?"

"Ah, a whole slew of people."

"What in the world does that mean?" Daniel strode to the window and looked out, too. And then he gaped. Standing just below the stairs leading up to his apartment was Nate, Lela and Lela's parents. Lela's *mamm* was holding a big basket and her father was actually smiling. "Why do you think they're here?"

"To see you, ain't so?"

"Thanks for pointing out the obvious."

"Anytime." He deposited his cup in the sink. "Come

over to the house whenever you want. My wife wants you to join us for supper."

He could hear everyone's footsteps on the wooden stairs. "Wait. You're leaving?"

"Of course I am. I'll just be in the way."

"No, you won't."

"You're gonna be just fine, Daniel Miller. I promise ya." Abraham patted him on the shoulder. "Now, go get the door."

Feeling a sense of doom that almost equaled how he'd felt when he'd first felt handcuffs on his wrists, Daniel opened the door.

Four smiling faces greeted him.

"Hiya, Daniel," Lela said softly.

She didn't look like she hated him. Neither did her parents. "Did you all need something?"

"We'd like to come in," Elam said.

He'd been blocking the door. He stepped backward as all four of his guests walked inside.

"We didn't know you had company," Charity, Lela's mother, said.

Abraham smiled. "I was just leaving."

"Everyone, this is Abraham Fry. I work with him at Carter and Sons, and he's also my landlord."

"It's good to meet you," Nate said as he shook his hand. "Nate Borntrager."

"I've seen you around," Elam said. "You belong to a different church district, don'tcha?"

"Jah." After saying hello to Lela and her mother, too, Abraham walked out the door and closed it behind him.

Daniel pointed to the small sofa and the pair of

kitchen chairs. "I don't have a lot of places to sit, but you all are welcome to sit down. I mean, if you'd like."

"Do you have any coffee?" Nate asked.

"Some." He ran a hand through his hair. "I might need to make some more, though." He turned to the kitchenette. "I'll do that now."

"Let me make it," Charity offered with a kind smile. "I need to get out the muffins I made for you, anyway."

She brought muffins? He was beginning to feel like he had stepped into another dimension. Realizing everyone was waiting for him to reply, he nodded. "All right."

Nate motioned toward the chairs. "Have a seat, Daniel. You look like you're about to collapse."

Since he rather felt like he was about to, he sat down on the sofa. To his surprise, Lela sat next to him. Daniel darted a look at her father, but Elam didn't seem concerned by their close proximity at all.

Ten minutes later, all five of them were holding fresh cups of coffee and had a pumpkin muffin perched on their laps. As good as the treat smelled, Daniel didn't think he could eat a bite.

At last, Nate spoke. "Daniel, last night when Mitzi and I took Lela home, we shared what happened with Elam and Charity."

Elam ran his hand down his long beard. "It was quite a story," Elam said.

"I'm sorry to put your daughter in danger." Unable to resist, he shifted slightly so he could face Lela. "I'll always regret what I did to you."

She frowned. "You regret saving my life?"

"Of course not. But we both know I didn't do that. I put you in danger."

"You didn't. Wyatt, or whatever his name is, did."

Nate nodded. "Lela's right, Daniel. Joey Stanton is the only person to blame for last night's events. Two officers interrogated him last night. He confessed everything. How he killed Brandt because he knew Brandt was going to tell authorities about his drug dealing. He went after you because you were there and knew that he'd been trying to recruit someone in the Amish community to work for him."

The detective's words made sense but it didn't mean he wasn't also at fault. "Still, I am very sorry, Lela. I would never want to ever put you in danger like that."

Elam cleared his throat. "Daniel, perhaps I should say a few words." Putting his empty cup on the floor next to his feet, he continued. "We didn't come over here to cast blame. We came over to say that we are mighty glad that you risked everything in order to keep Lela from harm."

"I told them about how you told Wyatt to kill you instead of hurting me," Lela added.

Elam's gaze warmed. "My daughter also shared that she loves you and that you love her, too. Is that right?"

"It is." Daniel had no idea where the conversation was headed, but that truth couldn't be denied. "I do love Lela."

Charity smiled brightly. "If you two are in love, we should probably start planning a wedding soon, *jah*? I mean, especially since you two were alone in the dark among the cornstalks for so long."

He felt like laughing. "I promise, I didn't compromise her. I mean, we were hiding…"

"I told *Mamm* all that," Lela piped up. "But *Mamm*

might have a point, you know. I mean, not every person in the community is going to believe that we never even kissed in the middle of the cornstalks."

"So you want to be married?" He felt like he was two steps behind.

Nate stood up. "Yeah, buddy. She wants to marry you, and her parents have given their blessing. Keep up."

"But I haven't asked."

Both of her parents stood. "We'll wait downstairs," Elam said. "How long do you think you'll need? Is ten minutes enough time?"

"Uh…"

"Let's give them a full fifteen minutes," Charity said. "This is a day Lela's always going to remember."

"Okay. I've got to eat my muffin, anyway."

And just like that, Nate and Lela's parents filed out, closing the door behind them.

Several seconds passed. Then Lela stood up. "Are you mad, Daniel?"

"What? No. Not at all." He set his muffin on the kitchen counter. "Lela, did you mean what you said? You still love me?"

Her pretty brown eyes shone. "I meant it. Did you mean it, too?"

"Every word."

She bit down on her bottom lip.

She was obviously waiting.

There was only one thing to do. He got down on one knee. "Lela Borntrager, you made my whole life better. You gave me light when all I could ever see was darkness. You gave me hope when I could only feel despair. I love everything about you, and nothing would make me happier than to see you the first thing every morning and the last thing every night. I love you with all my heart. Would you honor me and be my wife?"

"Of course, Daniel." She held out her hands.

He got to his feet, reached for her hands and kissed each of her palms. And then enfolded her into his arms, thinking that no other person would ever feel as perfect next to him.

And then, at long last, he kissed her sweetly.

Lela was his and he was a fugitive no more. He now had a home by her side.

Epilogue

One year later.

Just like it always did, fall had arrived once again. Sitting next to Daniel while he expertly managed Lucy's reins, Lela Miller wrapped her hands around her still-flat stomach as she gazed at the glorious fall colors. It was a lovely day. Although there was a bit of a chill in the air, it was still very agreeable, especially since the sky was such a vivid blue and the sun was warm.

Even though her husband had tried to convince her to wrap a thick blanket around her lap, Lela had refused, saying that her navy cardigan sweater would do just fine. She was glad that Daniel hadn't attempted to argue about it. He was coming to understand that she might heed his wishes about a lot of things but not everything.

Lela had to smile about that.

"You look like you just heard a joke. What are you been smiling about?"

"Nothing much. I was simply thinking about how we started talking about a year ago today."

Daniel's expression warmed. "That's something nice to think about, indeed."

"Do you ever think about all the changes that have taken place in the last year?"

"Let's see. I got out of prison, returned home, met you, got a job at Carter and Sons, settled back into Amish life, hid in a cornfield from a killer and then somehow managed to get you to fall in love with me? *Jah*. I suppose everything has crossed my mind a time or two."

She chuckled. "I guess that was a silly question."

"Not at all. We hardly talk about the past anymore. Maybe we should from time to time."

Lela shrugged. They'd secretly written some personal vows to each other before their wedding day and shared them in letters they exchanged the evening before. In Daniel's letter, he'd promised to be the man she needed him to be...and not allow himself to become bitter or dwell on being falsely imprisoned. In Lela's note, she vowed to be the wife and partner that he needed her to be, to help him find happiness in simple, everyday things and to try not to look back too much.

When they'd stood across from each other during the church service, Lela thought the vows they'd shared privately had been as special as the vows they'd exchanged in front of all their friends and family.

For the most part, they'd stayed true to their promises and settled into married life. After living in Daniel's garage apartment for several months, they were able to put a down payment on a house just a couple of miles from her parents.

And now they had a baby on the way.

"Daniel, next year, when we go for a ride, I'll be holding our babe."

He smiled. "We are truly blessed."

After another five-minute ride, Daniel directed Lucy up a gravel driveway and parked the buggy in front of a butter-yellow-colored cottage. Next to them was a silver truck. "It looks like Nate has already arrived."

"I'm eager to see him." She shifted.

"You wait there for me, Lela. I'll help you down."

She watched him easily hop down from the bench and walk around to her side. "You're being silly. I don't even have a big stomach yet."

"You are still carrying our wee babe." Curving his hands around her waist, he added, "Besides, this way I get a chance to give you a kiss and hold you close."

She felt her cheeks heat but didn't argue anymore. Her sister Ruth had given her some wonderful advice about marriage—that it was all about picking her battles. Ruth had pointed out that having someone who only yearned to make her happy and take care of her was something to be very thankful for, not complain about.

After she was steady on her feet, she gathered the pie server that had been on the floor of the buggy and waited while Daniel released Lucy from the buggy and walked her over to an empty field. They knew that she wouldn't leave on her own.

"You made it!" Mitzi called out as she walked down the cottage's front steps. "I'm so glad to see you."

"Me, too! Thank you for inviting us over for a picnic today." Lela hugged her hello as Daniel strode back to where they were standing.

"Good afternoon, Mitzi."

She inclined her head. "To you, as well."

"Where's Nate?"

"He's fussing with the grill on the back patio. See if you can help him, would you? It's been giving him fits today."

Amusement lit Daniel's hazel eyes, but he merely nodded. "I'll be glad to do what I can. Lela, would you like me to carry the pie holder for you?"

Oh, but the next seven months were going to be long, indeed. "*Nee*. I am fine."

"All right. I'll be around the back."

Mitzi looked like she was trying very hard not to burst out laughing as they watched him walk away. "Is he always like this, Lela?"

"Like what?"

"Uh, treating you like spun glass?"

"Only lately," she quipped. Realizing what she'd just said, she popped a hand over her mouth.

Mitzi's smile faded as Lela's comment slowly sunk in. "Only lately? What's… Oh, my word. Are you pregnant, Lela?"

She nodded. "I am."

Obviously looking at her figure from head to toe, her friend frowned. "It's impossible to tell how far along you are in that dress. How far along are you? Do you know?"

"Oh, *jah*. I'll be three months next week."

Mitzi's smile could've lit up a room. "Congratulations!"

"*Danke*."

"Oh, wait a minute. What am I doing?" She held out

her hands. "Give me that pie carrier," Mitzi said as she reached for the red plastic container.

"Why?"

"Because a simple congratulations just won't do." She gently removed it from Lela's grip.

Before Lela knew what was happening, Mitzi had placed it on the ground and enfolded her in a warm hug. "I'm so happy for you both. This is wonderful, wonderful news. I bet you're so excited."

"I am. I mean, we are."

"Daniel is over the moon, isn't he?"

Thinking of the way her husband had practically walked around with a permanent smile on his face the whole first week, she smiled. "Oh, yes."

"And your parents?"

"They're happy, too. But we've been trying to keep things quiet until next week's appointment. The midwife says that twelve weeks is a good milestone. You're the first person I've told outside of my family."

"I'm honored, then." Bending down, she picked up the pie carrier again. "Let's carry this out to the guys in the back."

Lela followed down the walkway. "You know, this conversation all started because Daniel was acting like I shouldn't be carrying a pie holder around. Now, here you are, doing the very thing he was trying to do."

"Dear, I'm sure you feel silly since you're young, healthy and strong, but my advice is that you simply enjoy getting a little bit of extra attention and help. Before you know it, you're going to have a baby in your arms or on your hip all day long."

Lela realized that, although she often chatted with

Mitzi whenever she went into BJ's or they saw her out with Nate, she'd never thought to ask too much about her private life. "Do you have children?"

"Oh, no. I just have a lot of friends and family who have a houseful."

"I'm sorry."

"Don't be sorry. I've made my peace with the Lord never blessing me with any, though it's probably just as well. My first husband was kind of a jerk. I'm glad we didn't have kids together."

"You were married and got a divorce?"

Mitzi turned to face her. "I did." Suddenly looking a little worried, she said, "I know you're not a fan of couples divorcing. I'm not, either, but after three years and hours of counseling, my husband and I realized that things weren't ever going to get a lot better. We really tried."

"I'm not judging you, Mitzi. I've just been realizing that I should've taken the time to know more about you. I'm sorry."

"There's nothing to be sorry about. You and Daniel have been really busy."

Lela reached out and squeezed her hand. "Maybe the Lord had a plan all along. You and Uncle Nate are so happy together. Why, if you had been married, you wouldn't have met Nate."

"You're exactly right about that."

When they turned another corner around the cottage, Lela couldn't help but gasp. The backyard was fenced, but just beyond it, the land started to slope until it reached a good-sized lake. "This is beautiful."

"I think so, too. One day we're going to get canoes.

You'll have to come canoeing." She bit her lip. "When you don't have two people to think about."

"You don't think I can canoe, either?"

Mitzi shrugged. "Just to be safe, I wouldn't do anything before you ask your doctor or midwife."

The men, who had been standing next to the grill, turned around. Her uncle's face warmed as he walked over and hugged her. "Hi, sweetheart. How are you doing?"

He looked so sweet and concerned, Lela blurted, "Oh, no. Did Daniel already tell you the news?"

Stepping back, he frowned. "What news?"

"Oh. Ah…"

Daniel shook his head in mock exasperation as he joined them. "Since Mitzi is looking like she is a cat who got all the cream, I'm guessing that you already told someone our secret, sweetheart."

"I didn't mean to. The words kind of slipped out." Maybe pregnancy brain was a real thing after all.

Her husband laughed as he put an arm around her waist. "I understand."

"I'm glad you do, because I sure don't," Nate announced. "What is this secret?"

Lela looked up at her husband. "Would you like to tell him?"

"Nope. I like to watch you share the news."

Nate groaned. "What news?"

Daniel laughed. "Lela, you'd best spill the beans before your uncle gets upset."

"I'm pregnant, Uncle Nate."

His expression softened as he hugged her again. "Now, that is some special news, isn't it? I'm very happy for you, Lela." When they separated, he reached out and shook Daniel's hand. "Congratulations. Babies are a wonderful thing."

"Thank you."

Looking toward Mitzi, Nate murmured, "It sounds like we have a lot to celebrate on this picnic."

"There's something more?" Lela asked.

"You could say that," Nate replied. "I think the pork tenderloin has a few more minutes, then I'll slice it and everyone can make their sandwich."

"What can I do to help?"

"You may sit down and relax, honey."

She turned to Mitzi. "Isn't there something I could do?"

Looking like she was trying not to laugh, she said, "Beyond rest? No."

Realizing that she was going to be surrounded by quite a few people who wanted to spoil her, Lela figured that there were likely lots of things worse than that. She sat.

Thirty minutes later, the four of them were sitting on a red-and-white-checked tablecloth, sipping sparkling water and eating pork sandwiches, potato salad and broccoli slaw. Two really beautifully made woven baskets nestled in the grass just behind the men. In front of them, the lake shimmered. A pair of ducks were lazily swimming in the center of it. It was peaceful and lovely. Lela couldn't imagine a better afternoon.

When they were almost done, Daniel spoke. "All right, I can't take the suspense anymore. Nate, what is your news?"

Lela's uncle reached for Mitzi's hand. "Mitzi and I got married two months ago."

Lela put down her plastic tumbler. "Two months ago? How? When? And why did you wait so long to tell us?"

"We didn't want to make a big deal about it," Mitzi said. "We went to the courthouse one afternoon and got married in front of a justice of the peace."

"Mitzi's sister and Jill, my friend from the force, stood up with us," Nate added.

"After, we went out to lunch."

Lela was happy for them, she really was. But she also felt a little dismayed. After all, she'd made her uncle promise to go to their wedding. "I see."

Nate continued. "We were going to go on a fancy honeymoon to a resort in the Caribbean, but this little cottage came up on the market. So we decided to buy this instead and spend as much time here as we could."

"Since I pretty much only saved all my paychecks while I was working at BJ's, I quit my job and decided to go back and forth wherever Nate is," Mitzi finished. "It's worked out great."

"I guess it has."

Daniel rubbed her back. "Don't worry so much, Lela," he said under his breath. "Can't you see how happy they are?"

Her husband's reminder was exactly right. Looking at Nate and Mitzi, Lela felt only love and happiness radiating from them. They weren't just happy; they were completely at ease. And so, so in love. Just like she and Daniel were.

Wasn't happiness and love and peace what really mattered, anyway? After everything that they'd been through in the last twelve months, Lela knew that none of those things could ever be taken for granted.

Realizing her mouth had gone a little dry, she took a sip of water. Then she gazed at three of the most important people in her life. Her heart was filled with gratitude and love.

At last, she raised her glass. "Congratulations and best wishes," she said at last. "Cheers!"

Chuckling, they clicked their plastic glasses and sipped.

"Thank you, Lela," Uncle Nate said.

Leaning against Daniel, she said, "Well, don't keep everything to yourselves. I want to hear all about this courtship. And how did Uncle Nate propose, Mitzi?"

Mitzi blushed as she started telling stories. Nate chimed in with additional tidbits, obviously eager to show that he could be charming from time to time.

Daniel asked questions and joked with them.

As for herself? Well, she savored the moment. It was a wonderful day.

* * * * *

Get 3 FREE REWARDS!

We'll send you 2 FREE Books plus a FREE Mystery Gift.

FREE Value Over **$20**

Both the **Harlequin® Special Edition** and **Harlequin® Heartwarming™** series feature compelling novels filled with stories of love and strength where the bonds of friendship, family and community unite.

Get 3 FREE REWARDS!

We'll send you 2 FREE Books plus a FREE Mystery Gift.

ONE NIGHT STANDOFF
NICOLE HELM

CONARD COUNTY
K-9 DETECTIVES
RACHEL LEE

HOTSHOT HERO IN DISGUISE

CAVANAUGH JUSTICE
DETECTING A KILLER
MARIE FERRARELLA

FREE
Value Over
$20

Both the **Harlequin Intrigue®** and **Harlequin® Romantic Suspense** series feature compelling novels filled with heart-racing action-packed romance that will keep you on the edge of your seat.

YES! Please send me 2 FREE novels from the Harlequin Intrigue or Harlequin Romantic Suspense series and my FREE gift (gift is worth about $10 retail). After receiving them, if I don't wish to receive any more books, I can return the shipping statement marked "cancel." If I don't cancel, I will receive 6 brand-new Harlequin Intrigue Larger-Print books every month and be billed just $6.49 each in the U.S. or $6.99 each in Canada, a savings of at least 13% off the cover price, or 4 brand-new Harlequin Romantic Suspense books every month and be billed just $5.49 each in the U.S. or $6.24 each in Canada, a savings of at least 12% off the cover price. It's quite a bargain! Shipping and handling is just 50¢ per book in the U.S. and $1.25 per book in Canada.* I understand that accepting the 2 free books and gift places me under no obligation to buy anything. I can always return a shipment and cancel at any time by calling the number below. The free books and gift are mine to keep no matter what I decide.

Choose one:
- ☐ **Harlequin Intrigue Larger-Print** (199/399 BPA GRMX)
- ☐ **Harlequin Romantic Suspense** (240/340 BPA GRMX)
- ☐ **Or Try Both!** (199/399 & 240/340 BPA GRQD)

Name (please print)

Address   Apt. #

City   State/Province   Zip/Postal Code

Email: Please check this box ☐ if you would like to receive newsletters and promotional emails from Harlequin Enterprises ULC and its affiliates. You can unsubscribe anytime.

Mail to the Harlequin Reader Service:
IN U.S.A.: P.O. Box 1341, Buffalo, NY 14240-8531
IN CANADA: P.O. Box 603, Fort Erie, Ontario L2A 5X3

Want to try 2 free books from another series? Call 1-800-873-8635 or visit www.ReaderService.com.

HARLEQUIN
PLUS

Try the best multimedia
subscription service for romance
readers like you!

Read, Watch and Play.

Experience the easiest way to get
the romance content you crave.

Start your **FREE TRIAL** at
<u>www.harlequinplus.com/freetrial</u>.